A BESS TRULY ADVENTURE

BESS TRULY
AND HER
ZAP-GUN
RANGERS

BY JOE SLEDGE

I0589884

North Carolina

Gravity Well Books

Publisher

First Edition 2020
Cover design by Barb Noel
Interior art by Chris Sheetz , Barb Noel, and Joe Sledge
Published by Gravity Well Books

For Callie

Contents

Chapter		Page
I	No Rest For The Weary	1
II	End Of The Deluge	7
III	Shake Rattle And Melt	17
IV	Not From Here	23
V	Nightfall	33
VI	Sabotage	45
VII	The Missing Man	51
VIII	Something Out There	59
IX	Who Goes There?	67
X	A Crowbar In The Plans	75
XI	Escape!	83
XII	Welcome To Three Winds	87
XIII	Breaking The Genie's Bottle	93
XIV	Fire On Approach!	101
XV	The Cavalry Arrives	111
XVI	Battle Of Fields Ranch	117
XVII	Cavalry Charge!	127
XVIII	The Desert Hunt	135
XIX	The Hard Way	143
XX	Hills Of Destruction	155
XXI	Dust And Moonlight	163
XXII	Annie Oakley Of The Sky	171
XXIII	Dancing By Starlight	181
XXIV	Battle In The Sky	193
XXV	The Round-Up	203

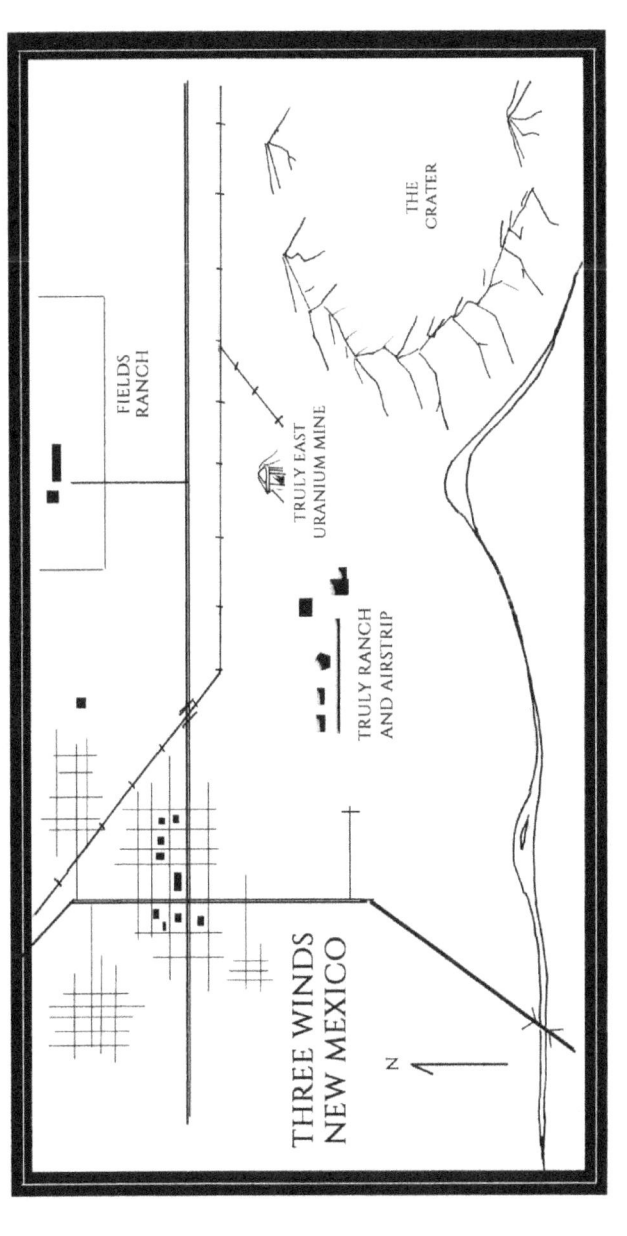

THREE WINDS
NEW MEXICO

FIELDS
RANCH

TRULY EAST
URANIUM MINE

TRULY RANCH
AND AIRSTRIP

THE
CRATER

N

Friday, May 11, 1956
Three Winds, New Mexico

CHAPTER 1

No Rest For The Weary

Bess Truly dangled her toes into a slow moving stream of water as she sat on the shaded riverbank. The water flowed from the west, out of a bright sunset over the open prairie that surrounded her hometown of Three Winds, New Mexico. The river was fed from rains on far distant mountains that poured into the river bed. Just outside town, the river curved into a wide arroyo, a sandy beach of shallow water where the kids from town came to play on hot days after school.

She sat under the branches of a stand of willow trees that dangled over the stream. Shade from the trees cooled her and a small cluster of horses that were tied to the trees. Her horse, Electra, stood with two other horses, a black and white paint horse and a golden palomino. They belonged to her two best friends, Aurora Baca and Lydia Lanier. The three girls had come to the arroyo after school, along with lots of other students, to cool off.

The setting sun meant it was getting late. Bess got up to get the horses ready to leave by packing up the towels and a small cooler of snacks and drinks the girls had brought. Off in the arroyo, Lydia and Aurora still splashed in the shallow water with their friend Jesse Armstrong. A year older than the fifteen year old girls, Jesse had driven his old orange dune buggy down to the arroyo and the four had played in the cool water until it was time for dinner.

Bess checked Electra's saddle one last time. Hanging off the horn of her saddle was her Zap-Gun. The Zap-Gun was an invention of her mother, Portia Truly, a physicist and electrical engineer. Two identical Zap-Guns hung from the saddles of Aurora's and Lydia's saddles.

The Zap-Guns were useful tools to have while working on a ranch, or traveling out onto the prairie. They could weld a wire to a fence post, make a bright flashlight, blast a hole into hard ground, and clear the dust from the air, among many other things. The girls took them everywhere. Her father Steve Truly had given the girls their nickname, the Zap-Gun Rangers.

Bess looked over the saddle of her horse toward the beach. Already, many of her schoolmates had left for home, driving off in their trucks and buggies, or riding back across the prairie on their own horses. There were about ten people left on the beach, besides Aurora, Lydia, and Jesse. Farther off into the river were two other girls. Nanette Fields and

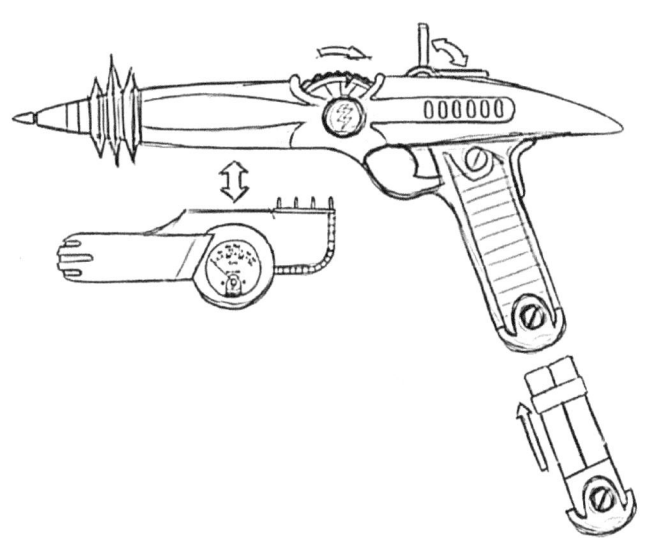

THE
ZAP-GUN
STATIC DISCHARGE DEVICE

SHOWN WITH OPTIONAL
GEIGER COUNTER ATTACHMENT

DESIGNED BY PORTIA TRULY, PHD

Annie Perez were standing on a gravel island that separated the little crescent curve of water from the deeper part of the river. Most of the kids stayed well away from the island. Occasionally older kids had bonfires out there. The fact that the burnt remains washed away after a storm was ample evidence that floods were dangerous and common occurrences.

The sun dipped behind a cloud. Bess felt the air go suddenly cool. She looked out to the west and saw the dark clouds of a storm that was rolling through the mountains. The rain was too far away to get them here.

Out in the distance of the river Bess saw an animal running through the river. A large elk ran down the sides of the river, splashing up the water as it dashed through the channel. It ran first toward the shallow beach, then turned away as it saw the kids playing in the shallows. It ran right across the island where Nanette and Annie were. The two girls watched the elk run by so fast they had no time to react.

For a moment, Bess followed the elk, too, as it seemed to run in a panic up against the bank of the river. It stopped, looked back, and began running again. Bess looked up the river at what the elk had seen.

Bess was the first to realize what was happening far upstream. She grabbed Electra's reins, pulling the horse from the tree while taking hold of her friends' two horses as well. At a run, she put her foot in the stirrup and leaped to her saddle.

Far out, all alone on the island, Nanette and Annie stood with their backs turned to everything and everyone as they watched the poor elk try to escape the river banks.

Bess had Electra at a gallop. She threw her holster over her neck and shoulder with one hand as she rode toward Aurora and Lydia. A roaring sound came echoing from far off, getting closer every moment. Somewhere to the west, a wall of water had poured down the mountains and had filled the river. The river then filled the arroyo.

Bess pointed up the river and screamed to Lydia and Aurora.

"Flash flood!"

CHAPTER 2

End Of The Deluge

"Get everyone to high ground!"

Bess yelled to Jesse while Aurora and Lydia climbed on their horses. Jesse ran to help some kids from a steep side of the arroyo. "I got'em!" he yelled. "Everyone, get out, the river's flooding!"

Lydia and Aurora were on their horses and looking around. Lydia glanced over her shoulder, "Oh, no! Nanette and Annie!" The three girls looked out at the island in the middle of the river. Nanette and Annie stood on the middle of the island, still watching the elk run down the river. They were unaware of the danger at their backs.

"We gotta stop that water from getting to them!" Bess commanded. "Let's go!" A tug of the reins and a soft kick sent their horses off like rockets, heading toward the danger. "Nanette! Get off the island! There's a flash flood coming!" Lydia screamed. It took a moment for Nanette to realize who was yelling at her, and what danger she was in.

Then they saw it, all of them. A wall of water churned from far up the river. It pounded against the distant banks and tore down chunks of sand and dirt. Bess drew her Zap-Gun and yelled, "Blast that bank!" A long outcropping of sand stuck out on the side of the arroyo. "We'll knock it into the river. It will slow down the water getting to the island until they get off!"

The three girls drew their Zap-Guns, Bess slinging hers out from across her chest and zipping the power wheel up in one motion. They pointed at the bank and squeezed their triggers.

Large blue blasts of zigzag lightning came out of the Zap-Guns. The sandy bank exploded into a cloud of sand and dust. Aurora rode her horse up to the dust cloud. She dialed her Zap-Gun down and fired. The sand was pushed into a long thin hill in the river. Bess shot a bolt of blue lightning into the sand, which made the hill tighten into a firm barrier. Small waves lapped at the new sand outcropping. The water washed around it. The new bank might hold for one big wave, but the girls knew it wasn't enough for the wall of water coming at them.

"Go get them!" Bess yelled to Lydia. Lydia wheeled her horse around and took off at a gallop. As soon as she turned, the first big wave hit the dune they made. The river pounded into the sand bank, but the waves were forced farther out into the deeper part of the river.

Lydia rode her horse onto the island without slowing. She simply ran her horse up to Annie and scooped her up with one arm. They turned toward the beach without stopping. Annie dangled on the side of the horse. She hung on to Lydia with one arm and onto the horn of the saddle with the other. Annie didn't care how she got to safety, as long as she got off the island.

Nanette screamed, "Come back! What about me?!"

Lydia didn't bother to answer. There was no way she could carry both girls at the same time.

As soon as Lydia got Annie to land, she heard a loud *BOOM!* and the big sand hill collapsed and disappeared under a wall of water. Now the river was getting deeper and flowing faster.

Bess felt the river deepen under Electra. Her horse fought to stay in place but the rising water pushed them back. Aurora was closer to the shore and better protected from the current. Bess was right in the middle of it all.

And Nanette stood alone on the island.

And the island was rapidly disappearing.

"Again!" Bess yelled to Aurora. The two didn't hesitate. They snapped their Zap-Guns down onto the wet sand, blowing it out in muddy chunks into the river. The sand wall had barely formed when a wave carried a large tree trunk up and over it, right toward Bess. She spun the dial of her Zap-Gun, then twisted once more with a solid click. It was on its highest setting. She aimed the Zap-Gun at the tree and squeezed the trigger.

A straight powerful blue beam poured from the Zap-Gun onto the tree. The thick trunk stopped in mid-air, fell back, and burst into splinters. There was nothing left of the tree as it hit the wet ground of the dune barrier.

"Nice!" complemented Aurora. Then she turned her Zap-Gun back to building the dune higher.

By this time, Lydia was heading back out to the island to get Nanette. The water was deeper, and her horse couldn't move as quickly through the flowing river. Nanette didn't help any by standing in the middle of the island instead of by the edge.

Lydia had to ride onto the island to get to Nanette. "Let me get on!" Nanette yelled. She tried to pull herself up onto the saddle, in front of Lydia. Lydia staggered to keep balance. "No! Over her back! What are you doing? Do you want to drown?" Lydia screamed back at Nanette, who was trying to take the reins of the horse. Lydia had to push Nanette back so they both didn't fall.

"Let me up!" Nanette screamed again. The rushing water was only getting closer and higher.

Suddenly, Lydia saw a bright flash of blue light. Bess had pointed her Zap-Gun at Lydia as a signal. It was time to go. NOW! Lydia saw the huge wave of murky water coming down the arroyo. No wall was stopping this wave.

Lydia didn't have time to fight Nanette on this. So she reached down and grabbed Nanette's long blonde hair and pulled. Nanette had no choice but to jump up and flop herself down onto the rump of Lydia's horse. The two rode in with water splashing up all over Nanette, just as the giant wave of water washed away the island.

Bess, Aurora, and Lydia made sure everyone was safe and able to get home. They didn't leave the arroyo until the sun had started to set and the sky turned orange. "Funny," Aurora had said, "We haven't gotten a drop of rain."

The prairie was like that, Bess thought as she rode home on Electra. Most people from outside the state pictured New Mexico as the Old West, with tumbleweeds and cactus growing out of the sand. But she knew better. The prairie was full of life, all interconnected. The flood would bring water for delicate flowers growing up under Electra's hooves. Whiptail lizards scampered from place to place as Bess rode home. They hunted the bugs that hopped and flew from plant to plant, then scurried off as Bess and her horse clopped through their hunting grounds.

She stopped for a moment to look around and admire the land that was her home. An orange sunset lit up the west. It cast its last light on Crescent Ridge, the low mountain range that stood to the east of her town. The mountains were old, with brittle and jagged spikes. Hidden deep within the mountains were mysterious caverns and caves.

To the south there were wide plains filled with elk and birds that filled the trees. Farther down in New Mexico were the ancient lava floes, the open gypsum desert, and the mysterious installations that had built and first detonated the atomic bomb more than a decade ago.

Bess took one last look to the west where the remnants of the thunderstorm wore itself out along the edge of the horizon. Then she looked north.

And to the north gleamed her home of Three Winds. It had been nothing more than a watering hole for travelers on stagecoaches until the roads had brought cars and vacationers on their way to California or Las Vegas. It had grown into a nice town, with a school, two parks, a movie theater and a radio station, as well as several restaurants and an ice cream soda fountain.

Tonight the lights from Three Winds had just started to twinkle on, as the sun set over the highway heading west. In between Bess and the town was a long line of buildings that blotted out the soft lights of the town and put out their own glow of bright, modern color. It looked like a Christmas tree on its side, with lines of green, red, and white stars shining brightly in the oncoming darkness.

This was Bess's family ranch, the C Bar M.

The C Bar M was built from nothing right out of the prairie by Bess's family, Steve and Portia Truly.

Steve had come to New Mexico after World War II, where he had been a fighter pilot, flying P-51s over Germany. After the war, he had come back to the U.S. and bought the land for the C Bar M with his wife, Bess' mother, Portia. She was a Doctor of Physics from the University of New Mexico. Portia raised Bess in New Mexico while working on secret electronics for the war while Steve fought the Germans.

When Steve came home, Portia went back to New Mexico University and got her PhD. in physics.

Bess woke herself from her daydream. The sky had gotten dark quickly. The lights of Three Winds stood out alone on the shadowy open plains. Bess wasn't scared. She had been out in the dark of night many times. And Electra was as sure footed as a horse could be. She could find her way home in the dark with blinders on.

Still, a little light wouldn't hurt, thought Bess. She pulled her Zap-Gun from its holster. Bess spun the power wheel to its lowest setting, pointed it forward, and squeezed the trigger.

A tiny arc of light came from the end of the barrel, reflecting into the glass circle. A soft blue light shone out onto the land in front of Electra. It lit up the ground for 100 feet in front of them. Her horse snorted, then started home at a confident trot. Electra didn't mind the Zap-Gun; She just knew she could get home to her stable without any help.

The stars began to come on, one after the other, until the sky twinkled like diamonds on a heavy black curtain. Even though there was no moon in the sky that night, the open plains were lit up by the light of stars.

Bess and Electra trotted on. They were only about a five mile ride from the ranch. She could easily see the long line of lights that marked her family's airstrip. Three low hangars holding her father's planes, along with a few other aircraft from town, dotted one end in a silhouette. One more hangar, bigger and not as square, stood over the other ones.

With her father being a pilot, and her mother a physicist and inventor, it hadn't taken them long to start working on a new type of aircraft. It was tucked neatly in the big round hangar, resting until it was ready for its first flight. It was going to be amazing, Bess thought, as she imagined it flying through the sky unlike any plane ever had.

Bess was startled from her imagination by the spotlight of the airstrip coming on and starting to spin. The light was a big aerobeacon, brighter than any lighthouse. The bright light could be seen for miles, especially in the flat prairie around Three Winds. No planes were coming in. The night sky was clear of any blinking lights. She realized the beacon had been switched on for her to come home. Her dad had turned the front porch light on for her.

Bess pointed her Zap-Gun up in the air toward the ranch and squeezed the trigger tighter. A bright flash came out the end. She let the trigger loose, and squeezed again. She was close enough that anyone outside on the ranch would easily see the bright light.

She waited, with Electra still slowly trotting toward the bright aerobeacon. Maybe her father would turn the light off or flash it back. He may just leave it on until she got there. Bess thought the beacon would flash back at her any second.

Suddenly, Electra stopped dead in her tracks. The horse snorted. She did not want to move another step for some reason.

"What is...?" Bess tried to soothe Electra with a pat to the neck. To the east, just over the low hills that rose up to form Crescent Ridge far off, a deep green glow flashed in the sky. It shimmered brightly, lighting up the night over the mountains for a split second.

That was when the aerobeacon went out. The beacon dimmed to yellow and then went dark. At the same time, all the other lights on the airstrip went out. And all the lights on the ranch.

And every single light in the town of Three Winds went out, too.

The whole of Bess's world went dark, except for the light of her Zap-Gun. Then the ground began to shake.

CHAPTER 3

Shake Rattle And Melt

Bess leaned forward in her saddle, holding on to the horn so she wouldn't fall off. She dug her heels into Electra's sides by reflex. The horse whinnied but wouldn't buck or move while the ground shook.

Then, everything stopped. The night went back to its dark starry sky. No green glow appeared over the mountains. It was almost as if it never happened.

Except that the lights were still off everywhere.

Bess gathered her wits. She was still on Electra. She still held her Zap-Gun in her hand. She had released the trigger so the light had gone out, but she hadn't dropped it in the dark, at least.

"Okay, Electra," Bess cooed to her horse, "It's alright now." She stroked Electra's mane to settle her. "Shoot, you seem calmer than I am," Bess remarked. "Are you good? Yeah? We need to get home, Electra." Bess gathered the reins. "Let's go, girl!" Quick as a whip, Bess spun the Zap-Gun on her finger and squeezed the trigger, while giving Electra a gentle kick. The two set out toward the ranch, with her Zap-Gun lighting the way.

Within moments, the lights started coming on. First the town lit up, then the ranch, and finally the lights on the airstrip came on, one by one, blinking down to the end of the runway.

Fifteen minutes later, Bess rode into the stables, while the entire ranch was alive like a swarm of bees.

She met her parents on the front porch of her house. They stood in the glow of headlights from a shiny new Jeep that was used on the ranch. The driver, their night ranch foreman, Joel, stood talking to her dad.

"Bess, thank goodness you're alright," gushed her mother as she gave Bess a hug.

"You okay, kid?" her father asked with his soft Texas drawl not softening the concern in his voice for his daughter. "I turned the light on for ya, but then it went out during that earthquake."

"So it was an earthquake!" Bess exclaimed. She had never felt one before. "I just saw that strange flash of green light."

Her parents stared blankly at her. They had been inside and hadn't seen anything like the green light Bess saw.

Her father stepped down from the porch and took her by the arm. "Listen, kiddo, we gotta go. There was a train derailment outside of town. The police think it might have caused the power outage, and we can get help there faster from here at the ranch than they can from town."

"And we need your help, sweetheart," Portia added. "We don't know if it's on the main rail or the spur line to our uranium mine."

Bess understood their concern. Her family owned the Truly East Uranium Mine. Far out on the edge of their ranch was a small uranium mine that only opened to the east. The wind blew across the plains from the west, north, or south, but never the east in Three Winds, so the mine was far away with little risk of radiation to the town.

After the United States began nuclear experiments, uranium mining became profitable, but extremely dangerous. Portia had made sure their mine was as safe as could be for both the town and the people that worked there.

What concerned Portia and Steve right at that moment was that they used a train on a spur line that ran to the Atchison Topeka Santa Fe Railway to move the uranium ore from the mine. If the train that derailed had been carrying the radioactive uranium, it may be spilled out all over the plains.

Portia ran back inside the house, just inside the screen door, and reached over to the coat hooks. Hanging there were two holsters, each holding a Zap-Gun. She ran back out as Steve jumped into the passenger seat of the Jeep.

Handing one holster to her husband, Portia said, "C'mon, Bess, we're going to need you out there if we have to help anyone."

Bess didn't wait. She jumped over the side of the Jeep and

into the back seat. The shiny new four wheel drive vehicle roared off as soon as she sat down.

They were the first to arrive to the scene of the accident. The Jeep could drive across the sandy prairie while any ambulance from town was limited to the roads and smooth paths. As Bess, Portia, and Steve got closer to the railroad line, they could see more clearly what had happened.

It was on the spur line, as Portia had feared. Bess could see the train engine still on the rails, pointed toward the cars that spilled out onto the gravel and sand that made up the foundation of the railroad. The engine had been pushing the ore cars from the end of the train. Nearby, a power transformer on a broken pole sparked and shorted in the near darkness. "Stop here, Joel," Portia said tersely.

She hopped out as the Jeep slid to a halt in the dust. Portia pulled out her Zap-Gun. She handled it by feel in the near darkness. She had invented the devices, so she knew how to use them well. Portia's was a little different. Hers had both the long static barrel and also a smaller sealed tube underneath with three vents on it that snapped open. Portia flicked the vents open with a click, then pointed the Zap-Gun outward.

It was a small Geiger counter that Portia had added to her Zap-Gun. It detected particles of radiation that might be present in the atmosphere. If her Zap-Gun sensed any radiation, the barrel would light up with a colored pop. Portia waited as she slowly waved the Zap-Gun around. It took about thirty seconds to finally make a tiny flash at the barrel. There was nothing but minor background radiation around.

"Órale, Joel," Portia said in a commanding but low voice, "You stay back twenty feet behind me as we approach. You watch me. If I tell you to stop, I want you to stop, and then start backing up. Don't wait for me."

"Yes, ma'am," Joel responded. He took Portia's commands seriously, especially since he had her daughter and husband in the Jeep with him.

They approached the wreck as fast as they could, with Portia leading at a slow run. Ahead, the engine sat in silence, with its headlight shining into the wrecked train cars.

Bess could just make out the familiar red, yellow, and silver color on the engine that marked the trains of the Atchison, Topeka, and Santa Fe railroad. They were seen all around the tracks of New Mexico. The bright light from the engine was almost blinding in the dark.

The light from the train blurred, as someone walked in front of the engine. Bess pulled her Zap-Gun, checked her dial, and shone a bright beam of light toward the figure. It was the train engineer. He walked around in disbelief, but seemed to be uninjured. The Jeep pulled up next him and the riders got out.

"Are we okay, here, hon?" asked Steve. She hadn't given him any sign of danger from radiation. The train cars that had tumbled off the tracks were hollow and empty.

"Yes, we're good. No radiation other than what we normally would get." She switched off the Geiger counter. "Are you injured, sir? Is there anyone else on the train?"

"I'm okay," the engineer responded, "The conductor is still up in the engine. He and our guard got banged up a little, but we're not hurt too bad." He looked down the tracks at the big empty black boxes that had tumbled off the tracks. "I don't know what happened." He scratched his head under his blue cap. "We were going ahead slow, then, wham, like we got hit with a baseball bat the size of a Sequoia tree. Didn't see nothin'..." he stared absently down the mess of cars broken and on their sides. "If we had been going any faster..." He shuddered at the thought.

Bess wandered down toward the empty train cars. The boxes were black, with large doors on the top to open for putting in the uranium. They normally would sit firmly attached to the flatbed cars. But now they had been ripped from their anchors by the wreck. All of the black boxes sat jumbled in the sand, like a giant had cast down toys from his train set. "What could have caused this?" she wondered.

Not far into the darkness, she discovered the origin of the crash, but it left her with no explanation, and more questions. Bess widened the beam on her Zap-Gun to take in the huge mess in front of her.

There she saw, rising up out of the sand and gravel, a strange and horrid sight. Twisted metal arms reached out from a dark pit, like some strange beast was trying to crawl out toward her from the very depths of the prairie.

CHAPTER 4

Not From Here

The entire railroad line had been blown up. The metal rails were twisted and bent. The ends split so badly that they looked like the arms of some giant steel octopus trying to wiggle its way up out of a coral reef. Only this wasn't a tropical ocean.

Bess looked at the scene before her. She counted the twisted and braided rails. Bess saw that the two rails had been split by a blast which made them poke upwards into four pieces. Each of those looked like they had then been frozen and shattered, which split the rails further into eight long shards. At the base of the carnage were the big wooden ties on which the railroad was staked. They were split into black splinters. The gravel and sand that was the base of the railroad was shiny, like an oozing mud bubbling up. It looked like the ancient lava flow at Carrizozo, but it wasn't black. The color and shape looked familiar. Bess just couldn't place it in the dark, with all the damage around. She tried to figure out what it looked like. She had seen something like it before.

"Mom!" she yelled, as she backed away slowly.

The three adults came running. Bess shined her light onto the mess in front of her. Her father looked at the big hole and said, "Well, I think we found the answer to the crash. Now, what in the world caused this hole?"

Bess had already thought past that problem. She said to her mother, "Mom, look at the ground. See, it's frozen, or melted. It looks a little like lava, but more like..."

"Trinitite," Portia finished. She pulled her Zap-Gun from its holster and turned the Geiger counter back on. The light at the end of the barrel did not emit even a spark. She slowly walked closer. Only when she was within a few feet of the area did her light start to pop softly. Portia took her belt off, looped it around the handle and trigger of her Zap-Gun, and unceremoniously tossed it right onto the melted sand. The Zap-Gun clattered as it bounced off the melted glassy sand. The barrel end lit up with a slow even popping sound as she pulled it across the glassy mound. "That's strange," she said, as she pulled the Zap-Gun back to her, and put her belt back on. "it's definitely radioactive, but even at close range, it's not giving off much. It must be sealed within the rock itself."

Steve looked from the melted blob and the twisted wreckage of the rail line, then up to his wife, and then back. Bess saw his breath come out as the air cooled into the dark night. He opened and closed his mouth without speaking. Then he finally formed the words, "How did this happen?"

The next day, the whole town was talking about the train wreck and not the flash flood. Bess had gone into town to meet Aurora and Lydia at the soda shop. The three girls were regular sights on the downtown streets every weekend. They had been best friends since they met in first grade. They were inseparable for the past ten years. Residents of Three Winds were used to seeing the three girls walking down the street side by side by side. Aurora had long hair, black as a raven's feather, while Lydia had a continual tangle of golden brown curls. The two contrasted well with Bess's strawberry blonde ponytail. All three were continually sun kissed by New Mexico's open blue skies, and they all sported tans and freckles. They walked into the soda fountain, laughing.

Jesse Armstrong's family owned the bright white ice cream shop, along with the local radio station and the theater. Mr. Armstrong had often said, "If we don't give our kids something to do, they will find something to do." He had put his money and his life into creating something fun for the people of Three Winds, and they had paid him back with their support. As the girls went inside, they saw Mr. Armstrong happily carrying huge tubs of ice cream.

"Hey, Mr. Armstrong!" Lydia said to the smiling man. "Stay cool, man!" she joked.

"Hey, girls," Mr. Armstrong replied. He wore a white paper cap that covered his close cut short hair. Whenever he grinned his glasses slipped down his nose. Mr. Armstrong usually had his glasses on the end of his nose.

"What's the special this week?" Aurora asked. Every week, Mr. Armstrong tried to have some new and strange ice cream or treat for townsfolk to try.

"Coconut Pineapple!" he exclaimed happily. "A taste of the tropics!" Ever since Hawaii became a tropical vacation land, everyone wanted a taste of the Pacific islands.

"Ooooo, that's for me!" Lydia cooed.

The big tub of ice cream thumped into the freezer. "Okay, Jesse will be out in a sec," Mr. Armstrong called to the back. "Jesse! Customers!"

Jesse came hustling out. He was in his soda jerk uniform, all white shirt, pants, and apron, with a cloth white cap with a thin blue stripe. "Hey," Mr. Armstrong stopped Jesse, "Where's your bow tie?"

Jesse touched his collar, then, with a mock surprised expression, patted his shirt until he found a tiny black tie in his pocket. "Okay, as long as you have it," Mr. Armstrong laughed as he patted his son on the back. "Enjoy, kids," he said as he left the shop. "Bye, son!"

"Hey, beans!" Jesse greeted his friends. "Whatta ya have?"

"I want that coconut pineapple," Lydia said as the girls sat down in a booth.

"Chocolate marshmallow mint," said Aurora.

"Rainbow, in a cone," said Bess.

The girls talked and laughed while plugging dimes into the jukebox to hear Elvis Presley, Patsy Cline, and Carl Perkins sing to them. The bell over the door rang as other people came in and out, to sit at the counter or get a cold drink on their way somewhere on a warm day.

The bell rang over and over until the girls no longer looked up to see who came and went. They didn't notice the two people who came in until they heard Jesse laugh and make a suggestion of a concrete, his special extra thick milkshake. Lydia looked up to see him leaning over the counter at Annie and Nanette sitting on the swivel stools. Jesse was smiling at Annie as he offered her a paper soda jerk hat. Annie rolled her eyes and perched it sideways on her head and smiled back at Jesse. "You think Jesse likes Annie?" she said.

"Jesse likes everybody," Aurora commented absently.

"Yeah," Bess added, "he's perfect for this job." Soda jerks had to be charming, funny, always happy, which described Jesse perfectly. "But, yeah, maybe. It would be nice for Annie to be around someone else besides just Nanette."

Nanette Fields was the daughter of James Fields, who ran a large beef cattle ranch to the north of town. Her family, while wealthy, didn't participate much in the town. Nanette tried to throw parties and do things that would show off her wealth, but she was often conceited to the other kids in school, so no one really liked to be around her. Annie had become her best friend when her family had moved to Three

Winds. Most people hoped that Annie would soften Nanette's mean streak.

Annie looked over her shoulder at Lydia and smiled shyly, and gave a soft wave. Lydia smiled back with her eyes and bright white teeth. Nanette looked over to who Annie was looking at, then pointedly turned her back to the girls.

Annie leaned over the counter and whispered something to Jesse.

A few minutes later, Jesse brought over a small glass of strawberry milk and a little sugar cookie on a plate. They were treats given to little kids or people having birthdays that came in to the shop. "Annie wanted me to give you a strawbaby and a cookie to say thanks," he said. Jesse called a glass of milk a "baby."

The three girls looked over at Annie, who turned again and mouthed, "Thank you," to Lydia. Lydia gave her a thumbs up and bit the cookie.

"That's pretty keen," Bess said between licks of ice cream.

The girls finished their ice cream, paid, and left. Full of ice cream and the rest of the day ahead of them, they went to the nearby park. They stretched out in the freshly mown grass and stared up at the deep blue sky while they talked.

"No one is even talking about the flood at the arroyo. Everyone is wondering how the power went out."

"My folks were watching Life Of Riley when the TV went off."

"I saw the whole town go out," Bess shared. "I was out on Electra riding home when it happened."

"That must have been a sight!" exclaimed Lydia. "I was just in the shower. It was weird, though. All dark like that."

"It wasn't entirely dark," Bess went on. "It was really nice, actually. The stars were just lit up all across the sky. You could see everything, and at the same time it was black as tar.

"I saw the funniest thing, though," Bess went on. "Right when it happened, there was this big green flash of light from far off."

"Like lightning?" asked Aurora.

"Kind of, but really intense. It was quick and bright, not behind a cloud or anything."

"Was it the train exploding?" asked Lydia.

"That's just it," Bess explained. "It looked like it came from the sky."

"And speaking of coming from the sky..." Aurora pointed up at the azure sky. A plane buzzed low overhead as it circled the town before making a line to the south where the airstrip for the C Bar M was. "Looks like you've got guests," Aurora said.

Bess looked up at the plane and recognized it by the V-shaped rudder as a Beechcraft Bonanza. The plane was popular with rich doctors, former fighter pilots, and the U.S. government.

Bess decided to go see which one landed at her home.

She said goodbye to her friends, reminding them to come to the ranch the next day for her flight, and went to get

Electra from the nearby stables that kept the horses in fan cooled stalls. By the time she had begun her ride, the plane had landed and disappeared behind the hangars.

It was a short hop back to the ranch. When she rode back in, she looked over at the airstrip to see the Bonanza already on the apron by the hangars. The pilot stood near the plane, wearing a military uniform and pilot's glasses. No one from the ranch talked with him as the pilot stood guard over the plane. With his short cropped hair, side cap, and green flight suit, Bess recognized him at once as an Air Force pilot. "Sure isn't any doctor visiting us," Bess commented.

Bess took Electra to the stables and made sure she was comfortable. As anxious as Bess was to see who was visiting them, her horse came first.

As she got to her home, she walked softly up the porch steps and into the front hall. She didn't want to disturb her family, but she was also hoping to find out who it was that came in on the plane. It had to be some sort of government people.

Voices came from her father's front office. Bess stopped to listen. She was surprised at what she heard.

"No, we don't know what caused the explosion on the railroad tracks. We can tell it had nothing to do with the train itself." Whoever it was speaking had a young confident voice, like a radio DJ. Bess didn't recognize it.

"Yes," came Portia's answer. "It doesn't seem to be an explosion. There is no way to get explosives down under the rail line that easily. Plus, we found traces of that radioactive glass sand up the hill. It's almost as if the energy was shot down from the mountain."

"That was our conclusion, too," said the Voice. "It seems like more of a ray or beam than a bomb."

"An atomic ray?!" This was Bess's dad. "Do we even have the ability to do that?"

"No." The Voice was adamant. "Our military cannot make an atomic beam ray."

"Well, who can?" asked Steve.

"No one," said Portia resolutely. "The Soviets, the Chinese, the British, Japanese. No one can do that."

"She's right," said the Voice. "No one can.

"No one on Earth."

CHAPTER 5

Nightfall

Bess froze at the words.

"No one on earth," the Voice had said.

Even more curious now, Bess moved toward the door of the office.

"You might as well come in. You're going to need to know about this sooner or later, Bess," said Portia through the open door.

Bess sheepishly walked into her father's office. "Mr. Truly..." Bess saw the man behind the Voice. He looked uncomfortable as Steve Truly smiled at him from behind his desk. Another man sat stiffly in an overstuffed leather seat.

"You two want our help, right? That's why you're here. Well, Bess is my copilot. She's part of the team," said Steve.

"And we trust her completely," said Portia.

Bess beamed at the compliment.

Portia closed the door to the office. "No more distractions for now," she stated firmly.

Bess took in the two strangers in the room with her parents. The Voice was tallish, thin, blond hair and pale pink skin. He looked decidedly not like anyone looked like in New Mexico. The Chair sat uncomfortably in the leather seat. He was... Bess tried to think, "He looks like he would be someone you would never notice. He's barely there." The Chair had black hair, a round nose, and there was nothing else that Bess could notice about him to make him memorable. The Voice was Elvis compared to the Chair, Bess thought.

Portia introduced the two men in suits. "Bess, this is Special Agent Phillips," Bess's mother pointed to the Voice, "and Special Agent Marsh," she waved offhandedly at the Chair.

"G-Men, huh?" Bess commented.

Her father smiled at the slang term. The two agents seemed to cringe slightly, but said nothing.

"So, you were sayin'," Steve prompted the FBI agents.

"Yes.. well..." Agent Phillips began.

"Not on Earth, you implied," prompted Portia. "Are you saying this is from another world?"

"You're not starting that Roswell stuff again, are you?" asked Steve. It had been almost ten years since rumors and newspapers had spread the word that an alien space ship had crashed outside of the town of Roswell, New Mexico.

Portia huffed, "Pfft, that was no space ship."

"Yes, we know," said Agent Marsh, speaking in front of Bess for the first time.

"I'm not going to have any 'little green men from Mars' stories popping up to cover any weird events," Portia stated.

"We aren't saying men from Mars, Mrs. Truly," Agent Marsh affirmed. "What we are saying is we don't know what this was, and we would like your help to find out."

Portia looked at the man, hard. Bess could see even her mother had a difficult time pinning the guy down. "If you say that no government currently can do this, but somehow someone did, then until I have evidence to the contrary, I'll listen to options."

Steve leaned forward in his chair. "So, what does that have to do with us, though?"

Agent Phillips joined back in. "Your new craft, the flying saucer,..."

"The Starlighter," Bess corrected.

"What?"

"It's not a flying saucer. It's not a space ship or a UFO. It's called the Starlighter."

"Your *craft*," Agent Phillips emphasized, "is ready for flight, correct? We are hoping you can use it for searching for any potential dangers. If there are enemies looking to disrupt our uranium supply, and they possess a weapon like this, we need to know where they are."

Steve stood up. He had designed the Starlighter, and Portia had invented the engine. It was their ship. Steve didn't want it turned into a weapon. "The Starlighter isn't a fighter plane, Agent Phillips. It's not armed. And it isn't a space ship that can fly to the moon like in the movies. It's not meant for that."

"We know that, Mr. Truly," said Agent Marsh. "We know all about the Starlighter. We just want you to help us. If you see or detect any strange events, all we want to know is where they are. Nothing dangerous, nothing risky. You leave that to us."

Portia didn't like the agents being involved in her project, but she didn't mind showing off her work.

"The test is tomorrow evening, if you would like to see it."

The sun had just begun its dip toward the horizon as the Starlighter was wheeled out of its hangar for its maiden flight. It was a major project for the entire family. The craft was unique in all of aircraft design.

From the outside, it looked like a flying saucer. But it was nothing like the UFOs that were part of popular culture now. It wasn't some strange craft from outer space with little aliens piloting it. It was new, fast, powerful, and light. It could manoeuvre in any direction, like a helicopter, but at a much faster speed, and far higher altitudes, and fly as fast as a jet. Or at least it should. Steve Truly wasn't sure just how fast it would go. He couldn't wait to find out.

The engine was Portia's invention. It worked in a similar way to her Zap-Guns, only at a much higher level. The center of the Starlighter was a large point of polished iridium. The shiny metal was incredibly dense and strong.

The center point worked the same way as a Zap-Gun, and when it fired, the tremendous electric static charge heated the underside and lifted the Starlighter off the ground. An outer ring of the Starlighter was also made of the iridium alloy. This outer ring spun at a high rate to keep the craft stable.

The middle ring was a wide flat disc divided into smaller blades that opened like a giant fan. They would remain closed as the craft lifted off, but would open slightly when the Starlighter was flying to control its direction. The fan wings surrounded the entire craft in a big circle, so it could move in any direction. When the power to the Starlighter ran out, or when it came in for a landing, the wings could all open at an angle and the Starlighter would slowly spin back down to earth.

The center part of the Starlighter was its cockpit. It was a dome of a special plexiglass in a metal frame so that the pilots could see in any direction. It was set on gyros to keep the cockpit separated from the rest of the craft. If the center was connected, the pilot and crew would spin madly and become too dizzy to fly.

Steve knew the design was foolproof, if nothing went wrong.

Bess and Steve walked around the Starlighter. They went over a long checklist of items to make sure everything was ready for the flight. It was a time honored tradition of pilots everywhere to check over their craft.

Finally, they climbed into the cockpit. Most of the craft was run electronically. The controls were designed by Portia, who had built them herself. The Starlighter needed electronic controls to work the many parts of the ship as fast as possible.

Most of the ranch workers had come out to see the take-off. It was going to be a beautiful sight to see, Steve had promised. Aurora and Lydia stood just outside the hangar. Bess had told them how the Starlighter would fly up in the air with the bright chrome ship making pops of light in the evening sky.

"See you when you land, honey," Portia wished to her husband. Steve would never admit being superstitious, but all fighter pilots were. He never wanted someone to wish for a safe flight. It might mean the opposite would happen. He smiled at her, and patted his pants pocket, where a lucky silver dollar nestled.

Bess had no lucky charms. She hadn't been flying long enough to find one. Her mother insisted her skill was enough to keep her safe. Bess liked her mother's confidence. And besides, she was just the co-pilot. Her father would do most of the actual flying of the Starlighter.

The aircraft already hummed with life as Bess and her father strapped themselves into their seats. After a quick last second check of their equipment, they were ready for take-off. Steve looked out the window toward Portia and gave her a thumb's up.

A more official signal was given by the ground crew to Steve. First, a single person in Steve's line of sight flashed a green flashlight beam at him, then ran quickly away. Next, Portia switched on a bright green light that was attached to the hangar frame above her head. That meant that Steve had complete control of the Starlighter.

"Let's go touch the sky, kiddo," Steve said to Bess.

Steve lifted a red cover and snapped a switch on. The Starlighter spun to life. The outer rim began whirling on its edge with a soft metallic whine. It felt like the ship was planting its feet to jump. The Starlighter was getting comfortable, Bess thought.

"Here we go!" Steve pressed the main engine button.

Immediately, Bess felt a rapid popping sensation, like she was sitting on top of a giant pot of popcorn going off all at once. The Starlighter jumped up in the air. It immediately flew higher than of all the hangars and shot up over 300 feet. She looked out across her windows and saw nothing but a soft orange sky out to the horizon. The sun was just setting in the west, and the eastern sky was turning into a beautiful purple twilight.

Steve slowed the ascent of the Starlighter by twisting back on the throttle handle. Bess felt the pops slow to a more agreeable rolling *thump thump thump*, like an excited heartbeat. The Starlighter was alive and happy.

Bess looked over at her father, who kept his hands on the controls and his eyes on the horizon. Right now, Steve stared out over the mountains to the southeast. "Everything looks good, right, Bess?"

Bess looked over the control panel. The Starlighter was flying great. It hadn't used even as much power as she thought it would to take off. The rotating wing was spinning fast and stable. The inner winglets were locked flat. The ship pulsed with power comfortably. "Looking good, Dad," she told him.

"So, what do you think? Up and out?" Steve raised his eyes to the darkening sky above.

"Up and out," Bess agreed.

Steve angled the Starlighter slightly by dipping his control stick, then twisting the throttle up. The winglets opened slightly with a soft *clackclack* and the Starlighter lifted up toward the darkening sky above.

Down below, everyone watching at the ranch would see the ship become smaller and smaller against the purple sky. Stars were just starting to twinkle on in the heavens above. The Starlighter made her own twinkle of light with every pop of her engine. Brighter than any star or planet in the sky, the Starlighter blinked out a bright blue light, which was visible to anyone looking up at the ranch, the town, or for a hundred miles in any direction.

Bess didn't see any of that, sitting in her seat in the Starlighter. And she didn't care. She was flying high up into the sky. The sun had begun to caress the edge of the horizon. The entire western sky was made up of lines of color, from yellow to orange to red all the way to purple. She saw Venus

shining brightly, but not as bright as the Starlighter, Bess thought. At this height, Bess wondered if she could see all the way to Utah, or Texas, or Arizona.

"Looky that!" Steve was so happy to be flying that his accent slipped into a deep twang. "We're so high up you can see down onto Crescent Ridge!"

Bess had never been this high in the air before. The details were lost and the whole prairie opened up in grand views from this altitude. She could see the glowing west sides of the mountains and the darkened east side, hidden in shadow. The trees of the plains looked like pins in a map, but their shadows reached out incredibly far. They looked like long thin dark hands with narrow fingers reaching toward the darkened east.

To the north, Bess could see Three Winds and the C Bar M Ranch. The town lit up with soft spots of light and bright colorful neon. The ranch had tiny pinpricks of light around her home and the bunkhouses and barns, while the runway and their takeoff area on the tarmac were lit up with a circle of white lights so they could easily find their way home.

After twenty minutes of flying, Steve asked Bess, "How's our fuel, uh, power level?" Flying on a stored electric charge was different than his old P-51 Mustang. He was still getting used to the new terminology. Bess checked her control board.

"We have a good twenty minutes of regular flight left, plus our reserve."

"Okay, that's good enough for a first flight. I don't want to test our glide recovery on this flight. Let's head back. You take the stick and collective to get us home."

This was the first time Bess had control of the Starlighter. She knew all about how to fly it, but since it was the first time up for the aircraft, no one had flown it before. She dipped the craft to the east. Because it was a disc, the Starlighter had no true nose or front. It flew where ever the pilot said. Bess held the Starlighter in a slight angle, which allowed her to see more of the ground under the ship, including the nearby mountain range. Bess was distracted for a moment as she looked into the dark shadows of the mountains that made up the Crescent. The ridge line curved, creating the crescent shape that gave it the name. The darkened inner part of the Crescent was called The Crater. It was a half moon shaped basin of old jagged rock edges. Bess saw something that caught her eye. She thought something moved in the shadows.

"Keep your head in the game," her father said, with a soft tone. He knew how easy it was to get lost up in the air, and how wonderful it felt to fly through the sky, without a worry on your mind.

"Sorry, Dad," Bess apologized, "I just thought I saw something in..."

Her next words were cut off as a bright green blast of energy shot up out of the Crater. An explosion outside the ship shook the Starlighter, sending it tumbling out of the sky.

CHAPTER 6

Sabotage

Bess immediately yanked the control stick hard away from the flash. The whole aircraft shook. Bess felt her teeth rattle as the explosion rumbled just outside the Starlighter. The Starlighter dipped down toward the west, and its air cushion spilled out from under the skirt. Bess twisted the throttle, pushing the power up to full. She was trying to keep the Starlighter flying and get it away from the mysterious green blast that had happened over the mountain range.

Lights started flashing and a loud warning buzzer began beeping. The Starlighter was at too much of an angle, and was falling fast. "Something happened to our power supply!" Steve yelled. As if in answer, a crackle of blue light and a thump occurred under the ship. "I think that blast got a piece of the battery."

"It's okay, it's okay! We have to get lower anyway," Bess yelled back.

Her father struggled at the weird angle to reach a switch and turn off the beeping warning siren. They already knew they were in trouble. He didn't need the noise to remind him now. "No, go to full power and get us out of range!"

"We need to get below the mountain edge," Bess wasn't sure what had caused the explosion, but she had this feeling the threat came from below them, and it was hidden in the darkness of the Crater. The sheer cliff range would act like a shield if she could safely get low enough. She just needed to get the Starlighter straightened out.

Bess twisted the throttle control down, then shoved the control stick hard sideways. The Starlighter was flying away from the blast, and angled steeply down. The winglets on the trailing side of the ship opened, and the front ones, the leading edge, closed. Air rushed through the back and lifted the front, which helped straighten the Starlighter. They were now at only five hundred feet, but they were level and moving away at a fast pace.

The rest of the winglets closed with a loud clank.

"Okay, I'll take her, Bess," her father insisted. "Good flyin', cowgirl."

Bess sunk into her seat after letting go of the stick and throttle. She couldn't tell if it was the Starlighter's heart that was pounding, or hers.

Seconds later, she could tell it was only her heart beating. That stopped for a moment as well, when they realized that all propulsion had run out on the Starlighter. It flew on, eerily quiet.

"Alright, I guess we just became a glider," Steve said. He yanked the emergency landing lever. The lever would send an electronic signal to all the winglets to open at forty five degrees. The air would push through, which would then slowly spin the Starlighter down to a landing. Underneath them, the giant gyroscope that helped keep the ship stable would whir until they were safely on the ground.

Only, there was no opening of the winglets. They all sat flat as the Starlighter continued to glide back to the ranch, while headed down, faster and faster.

Steve yanked the release again.

Nothing.

Bess tried hers.

She got the same result.

"This shouldn't happen," Steve thought. There's no way that can go wrong." He had only a split second to wonder. The Starlighter was going down, and fast.

As a last resort, Steve stuck his foot under a covered switch on the floor. He stomped on a big silver button embedded in the metal. It was a simple device. This was his ultimate, last ditch save yourself design that he had put in. Wires ran from the big button to small boxes at each winglet. The boxes held a simple device that ignited a charge, which then exploded a shotgun shell at each winglet. Every locked wing popped open with a bang.

The Starlighter immediately slowed and began to spiral quietly to the ground. Steve looked at his altimeter and did some quick math. They probably would land more softly than if they used the engines.

He would have been right, too, if the Starlighter hadn't landed on top of a tree.

By the time the trucks rolled from the C Bar M and had gotten to the crash site, Bess and Steve had already crawled out and were sitting on top of the canopy, counting stars. "And that's our lucky one, right there," her father said.

It had taken the rest of the evening to bring in a crane and a truck large enough to carry the stricken Starlighter back to the ranch. Ranch hands worked feverishly to lay out a mile of Marston Mats, big steel sheets with holes in them that could be laid across the soft ground so that the flatbed truck with the Starlighter on top would not sink into the sand as it crossed the plains back to the C Bar M.

Even though it was nearly 1:00 a.m. by the time the Starlighter sat back on the apron of the airstrip, Portia was not about to go to bed. No one was sleepy after all the strange events of the past evening. She crawled into the cockpit to figure out what had happened to the controls. It was her design that ran the Starlighter. The winglets should have released properly. "It's impossible for them to fail," she repeated what her husband had said earlier.

Steve knew from past experience that in flying, it was never really impossible for something to go wrong. Highly unlikely, like being hit with a giant green explosion, but nothing was impossible.

He still knew it was better not to argue with his wife. She was right, anyway. The winglets should have released when he threw the emergency release landing lever.

"Look at this," Portia climbed out from under the open panels where she had been nestled while looking at her wiring. An open diagram book of her electronics lay at her side. In her hand was a thick electric connector plug. Shiny black tape hung loosely around one end. "Here's the problem. The main communicator wire from the release to the wings came unplugged."

Steve looked at the plug. He pulled at the unraveling tape. "Did that blast cook the wire wrap? It looks like it came undone."

Portia shook her head. "That's heat sealed wrap, not regular electrical tape. It would melt into the wire instead of shredding like this."

So, if it didn't melt, and it didn't unravel, how did it come apart?" Bess asked.

"It was cut," Portia stated firmly.

"That means…" Bess took in a deep breath when she realized what she was saying next, "someone tried to sabotage the Starlighter!"

CHAPTER 7

The Missing Man

For the next week, the world came crushing in on Bess and her family. The whole town was on edge and concerned. They had seen the Starlighter fly into the twilit sky only to look like it had been struck down by a strange bolt of lightning far out in the prairie. Everyone feared the worst when they watched the ship go down into the empty plains. It wouldn't be until the next day that most of the citizens of Three Winds knew that both the ship and its crew were relatively unscathed.

Bess still couldn't believe she had experienced the strange explosion out of the dark sky over Crescent Ridge. Or that someone on the ranch tried to sabotage the Starlighter and possibly kill her and her father.

Steve Truly immediately described the explosion to Agents Marsh and Phillips. They seemed less surprised than Steve thought they should be. The G-Men had wanted to keep the news of the strange blast quiet, but Steve pointed out that everyone had already seen it, so there was no way to cover up what had happened.

"At least don't talk to anyone about it, Mr. Truly," Agent Phillips had insisted.

"Well, since I don't know what it was, I don't know what I'd tell them anyway," Steve replied.

The sabotage of the Starlighter was a more difficult issue to deal with. Portia went over the Starlighter wire by wire to determine if anything else was wrong. The only thing she could find was the emergency landing release. The heat sealed wrap had been cut and peeled back over the connector plug, and the wires separated. It was obvious that it had been done purposefully.

Portia was doubly concerned. Having the emergency release cut would only be a problem if the Starlighter had to land without power. The only other way to use it was in a test. She knew that Steve didn't plan to test the emergency landing technique on the first flight. Did the person who cut the wire know that the Starlighter would be damaged or attacked? Did he or she just think they would test the emergency landing on the first flight, possibly at a lower altitude? What was the intention of the sabotage?

Portia had been going over who could have done it. The engineers she had working with her to build the controls all had a stake in its success. No one would want to see their work fail. She knew all of them from her work at Los Alamos in the past, and trusted them.

The ground crew worked on all their aircraft. That was a bigger issue. There could be more problems with the other airplanes at the airport, which meant more checking, and more diligence against sabotage. Portia couldn't believe someone at the ranch could do such a thing. Most of the hands had been with them for years, especially the ground crews that worked on the planes and the Starlighter. They had come from military and passenger airline backgrounds, and they seemed happy. While there were only a few of them that actually went aboard the Starlighter, any one of them could have snuck on sometime in the night and done the damage.

It was quite a puzzle. Portia was very good at puzzles.

Portia had Bess gather all the logs on who was working the days before the incident. They also made a list of anyone who would have had access to the Starlighter. It was a pretty big list. Almost anyone working on the C Bar M could have gone in to the hangar to see the Starlighter. But, Portia reasoned, there had to be more to consider. Whoever did it had to know what they were looking for, and have the technical skill to figure out where and how to damage the electronics. Portia discounted her engineers from Los Alamos. They were already screened by the government and had Top Secret clearance. It had to be someone who got on the ranch, or someone who worked on the ranch.

Bess looked at the list. Someone on there tried to crash the Starlighter, with her and her father on it.

"This... this just doesn't make sense, Mom," Bess said. "Why would someone do this to us?"

Portia stopped her intensive scan of the names of people she knew and trusted. Portia and Steve Truly had been through issues like this in years past. Many had been even more serious. Portia had seen spies working against the United States where she worked. Steve had been shot at and had risked his life for the safety of not only the U.S., but many other countries, too, during the war.

Bess hadn't been through all that. Portia realized that as daring and brave as her daughter was, she was still a teenage girl.

"This is a real trial by fire for you, isn't it, hon?" Portia said softly. She hugged her daughter. "We've let you take risks and learn lessons since you were real little, and you've done us proud. It's okay to be a little scared, confused, and angry. Don't feel bad if you don't know how to act with all this. When you know something bad can happen, you can deal with it. You may not want it to happen, but in your head, you're thinking about what to do if it happens.

"When someone you trust turns on you, that's much harder," Portia knew all too well what that was like. "Just remember, in those cases, it's not how you act that matters. It's how you react."

"Thanks, Mom. Thanks for trusting me."

"I have no doubt in you, or your friends, Bess. You are just like your father, running toward danger to help someone.

And you're just like me, because you're smart enough to fix anything," Portia smiled at her own compliment.

"Now, let's look at this list. We are looking for means, motive, and opportunity. All the people on the list had some opportunity, but many of them would have been noticed if they actually went on board the aircraft. It could have been any of the five airstrip crew or mechanics that were there in the past two days. It could have been Sterling, my engineer," Portia mentioned the assistant, Sterling Crane, with whom she worked in designing and preparing the propulsion system.

"Sterling?" Bess asked. "Really?"

"We'll get to that," Portia promised. She continued. "Any three of our ranch foremen, Manny, Joel, and Kenneth, would be able to go there without being noticed. They all did regular labor on the craft." Joel was their regular night foreman for the ranch. He had been with them the longest, since he was a teenage cowboy. Manny was the newest. He had come from a small cattle ranch in Arizona. He ran the day shift, and seemed capable, but Bess didn't know him well. He was quiet and rarely spoke to her. Bess knew he was having some problems getting to know the workings of the ranch. Kenneth worked weekends and vacation time for Joel or Manny. He had mostly worked in various ranches and as a manager of a cattle processing company.

"Finally, we have Agents Phillips and Marsh," Portia ticked off the names on her paper.

"The G-Men? Why would they be suspects?"

"We don't know who they are. They're wildcards. Especially that Marsh fellow."

"He did seem strange, like you barely notice him, but he could kind of make you trust him," Bess shook the strange feeling off her back with a shiver.

"I've got a call in to some friends in Washington. I'll find out more about them soon," said Portia. "Now, like I said ... we know who had the best opportunity, but who had the motive. Yes, Sterling had the opportunity, but would he like for the Starlighter to crash? He had a lot riding on its success, but at the same time, he could take the design and use it himself.

"Though I strongly doubt he did any sabotage. Our success would be more valuable to him than our failure."

"So who would have motive?"

Portia thought for a moment. "That may be the solution. And the most difficult question to answer. No one had any clear personal motive to do this. That means there was an outside pressure. In the language of you kids, someone put him up to it."

"How do we prove that?"

Portia shook her head. "That won't be easy. So we move to the next step. Gather evidence. You go check the foremen's bunk houses, and I'm going to head to the hangar."

As Bess left her house, she heard the phone ring in the office. Her mother picked it up, but Bess was already on her way to the small cottages used by the foremen.

She went to Joel's first. Bess knocked on the door, thinking he may be asleep, since he worked nights. The screen door was closed, but the wood door that would normally be locked was partially opened. She pulled the screen door out with a screech of the spring. "Joel?" she called.

No one was inside. Bess walked in. The place was a familiar mix of neat and cluttered. Joel rarely had a mess, but he often left things out. A book was open on a small table by his only cloth chair. His bed was made and neat. Dress cowboy boots sat at the foot of the bed, by his footlocker, but no other clothes were out. In the small kitchen, there were only a plate with the remnants of a lunch from the day before and an empty glass soda bottle.

Bess was about to leave when she decided to look in Joel's small wooden locker where he normally kept his work coat, gloves and boots. She opened it up to find it empty, except for Joel's pocketknife. Bess picked it up, and noticed it was sticky with some sort of tacky glue. She opened it to find more of the sticky glue on the blade. And close to the hinge was a tiny strip of black tape, just like the heat sealant used on the electric wires of the Starlighter.

The screen door screeched again. Bess quickly tried to close the blade and hide the knife as Manny walked in.

"Oh, uh, hi... Ms. Truly," Manny looked at his feet. He still wasn't sure how to address the bosses' daughter. Bess could tell he was suddenly as uncomfortable as she was in the small room. "Have you seen Joel?"

"No," Bess said. "I came here looking for him, but he's not here. Why, have you not seen him?" Bess became concerned.

"No, ma'am," said Manny, now a little more animated. "He was working last night, out on the south. We had some fencing over by the stream that ... well," Manny thought he was wasting time. "Ms. Truly, ma'am, it's just, I haven't seen Joel since yesterday day. He didn't come back last night."

Bess pulled Manny out of the cottage into the open. "Are you telling me Joel is missing?"

CHAPTER 8

Something Out There

Bess was a star at school the whole week. She wanted to tell how beautiful the world looked from up high. She wanted to describe what it was like to fly the Starlighter into the sky and light the night up. Instead everyone asked her how it had crashed. She had to suffer through whispered accusations about her and her father. Aurora overheard Nanette pretending to talk quietly to Annie, saying, "I bet she just doesn't know how to fly. She probably crashed it." Lydia and Bess had to convince Aurora to let it go.

"She just wants to make a scene," said Lydia. "She's hoping to get a reaction. That's why she said it so you could hear her. If you go fight her, she gets to be the victim, and she can accuse Bess out loud afterward."

"Just leave her alone," Bess agreed. She didn't have the strength to worry about what someone like Nanette thought.

Bess couldn't talk about the sabotage until they knew who caused the problem. After the second time of explaining that the Starlighter performed correctly, it just landed on a tree in the dark, she just gave up and shrugged it off. Almost everyone else in school knew she wouldn't do anything to ruin her family's invention, and the few that still talked behind her back, well, she knew she couldn't change them, and didn't really care.

By the end of the week, most of the town had forgotten about the events of the last Sunday. Bess had bigger plans, too. She gathered Lydia and Aurora into a quiet group at the end of school. "Hey, you want to go exploring? I want to go out looking for something. It's probably going to be an overnight."

Aurora beamed with delight. "I'm in. Wait, where are we going?"

Lydia said, "Like it matters. Let's do it. But, where *are* we going?"

"Crescent Ridge," Bess said softly.

"The Crater?" Aurora asked. "That's a long ride. We definitely will need to go overnight, and even then, that's a lot of time on horseback."

Bess thought. It was a long way, but she was really curious about what had happened in the Starlighter right before everything went wrong. She just wanted to see if there was anything she could discover that might be hidden out in the prairie.

As she thought, she saw Jesse heading out to the parking lot toward his dune buggy. "You want to ask Jesse? He can take us in his jalopy. He always wants an excuse to go off the roads in that thing."

The girls cornered Jesse in the parking lot and asked him. "Sure! I've been waiting for a good weekend to head out exploring. My dad's had me working every Saturday for the past two months, and he said I could have some time off. I think he just wants me to get out from under his feet."

The next morning the four kids met at the ranch. Since they weren't taking horses, Bess was able to pack some extra supplies and food into Jesse's old Ford.

Bess's father came out to look at the crew gathering around the car. "What adventures are the Zap-Gun Rangers off on today?" he smiled as he inquired where they were going.

"We're headed east," Bess said. "We're going to go check out the caves over by Crescent. It's too long a ride for us on the horses, so Jesse's driving us."

Steve walked up to Jesse and slugged him in the shoulder good-naturedly. Steve loved the boy, in part because he saw so much of himself in the adventurous youth. Steve had coined the name 'Zap-Gun Rangers' for all four of them, but Jesse never really coveted one of Bess's Zap-Guns. When offered one, Jesse had pulled out his long handled shovel from his dune buggy and said, "That's okay, Mr. Truly, I've already got my favorite tool." He had grinned and called it his 'desert crowbar.' "This will get me out of any trouble I get into." After that, Steve trusted the boy on the spot.

"We'll be on the west side of the ridge, where the river turns. We should be back before dinner tomorrow," Bess yelled as they spun their way out of the ranch in Jesse's noisy orange car.

The morning sun warmed the four kids as they ran the car down the pink asphalt highway that led through Three Winds and connected them with U.S. 66. The sky was tall and open, all deep blue sky as far as the eye could see. Aurora's hair blew out wildly from the front seat. She tried only once to hold it down, then gave up and let it fly into the onrushing wind. The old Ford's radio tried to play over the roar of the tires on the road and the wind in their ears. Through the speaker Kay Starr belted out *The Rock and Roll Waltz* as loud as she could, but couldn't quite make herself heard. The kids didn't care. They sang along anyway, knowing the words by heart. Without missing a beat, the radio station played straight into Elvis Presley's new hit, *Heartbreak Hotel*. Lydia rolled her eyes like she was in a trance. She thought Elvis was dreamy.

For a moment, Bess didn't have to think of the past week, of the Starlighter being damaged, or what she might find at Crescent Ridge. She stuck her head over the side of the car and let the wind roar into her ears until she could hear nothing but the wonderful dull sound, like a churning and unforgiving ocean, unrelenting waves on a shore.

The road was mostly empty as the four kids sped down the blacktop. Every once in a while, they passed a car heading into town from somewhere. The girls stood up and waved, like they knew the drivers coming in from somewhere else. The other cars, polished new sedans and coupes with the new styles of soft pastel colors and bright chrome, looked otherworldly and alien compared to the old 1930s buggy. Inside the cars, for a fleeting moment, they could see the driver and passengers. A dad sat upright at the wheel, his city hat perched on his head. The mom looked out the window at the empty prairie of New Mexico. She was hidden behind a stylish kerchief tied over her head, and thick white sunglasses that contrasted with bright red lipstick. Somewhere in the back kids would bounce in the seats, arms hanging out the windows as little hands waved back. As the cars flashed by, the driver would touch his hat, the mom would smile, and the kids would twist to look out the back window as the old Ford roared by.

Each of the cars were going on an adventure, but neither one knew where the other was headed.

The road trip had to end, Bess realized. What would have taken them hours on horseback through the heat of the prairie only took about forty five minutes in Jesse's jalopy. He slowed to turn off the paved road and point his dune buggy toward the rolling hills that stretched out before Crescent Ridge.

Once the dune buggy got off the hard road, Jesse and his car were in their element. It floated across the soft bumpy ground and flew easily up the hills and dunes.

"How come this thing is so much more comfortable on sand than it is on the road?" Lydia yelled.

"My tires are filled with water!" Jesse yelled back. Then he grinned at Bess. He always told Lydia strange stories about his car to see if she would believe him. "I'm just kidding! The tires and suspension are made to work better off road, and you don't feel the bumps as much. We also are going slower over soft ground." Jesse whipped the car into a tight turn, kicking up sand while the girls squealed with delight.

After driving around for a half hour, Bess suggested they head to their campsite near the river bend. It was a flat sandy beach near the base of Crescent Ridge. A short but steep hiking path led up to the ridge line where they could see into the other side of the ridge. The mountains were riddled with small caves and caverns all along the range.

"So," Aurora said to Bess as she pulled the bedrolls from the back of the jalopy, "What's your story, morning glory?"

"What's your tale, nightingale?" said Jesse and Lydia at the same time.

"Okay, I gotta tell you something, but you got to keep this one secret." Aurora made a quick cross over her chest as Bess continued. "Right before we had problems with the Starlighter, there was this big energy spike. From outside."

"Like, a lightning bolt?" Jesse said, surprised. There was no storm that night.

"No. Listen, something made that explosion on the train tracks. I think the same thing shot at me. And I think it came from the other side of the Crescent."

CHAPTER 9

Who Goes There?

The kids set up camp and got out their lunch. The four sat under a willow tree that hung over the bend in the river. As they ate cold sandwiches from a cooler, Bess filled them in on the events that happened when the Starlighter was attacked and fell. She explained about the sabotage and how Joel the foreman had disappeared. "I'm not sure what we are looking for. Just clues or signs of something or someone being out here."

"You think Joel was responsible for the sabotage?" Jesse asked in between bites of his food. "I can't believe he would do something that dangerous, trying to kill you and your dad."

"I can't believe it, either," Bess agreed as she shook her head. She looked over a geographic map they had gotten from the airport. It didn't show where the caves were, but they had a good idea of the height of the hills they would climb.

"I hope we have enough food," said Aurora as she lifted a flat rock with her toe to see what might live underneath.

Lydia snorted and laughed. "We're only an hour from town. We could drive back tonight for ice cream if we wanted to!"

"I'm just saying, if we are out exploring, I don't want to be starving out in the mountains all night."

"I just don't want to be out in the mountains all night," Jesse commented.

"I think it would be fun!" Lydia added to the back and forth banter.

"We won't be out all night, not if I can help it. We're just going to look for clues to what might have caused these explosions," Bess said firmly.

"Well," said Aurora, "I'm going prepared." She grabbed a bag of peanut M&Ms from their picnic basket of treats. The snack was still new and unique to the little town, even though it had been around for two years.

They waited until late afternoon to start exploring. Before they left, Jesse tied a small battery operated lantern with a red light to a tree, then ran the thin string around a bottle he filled with water, and tied it to his car. "I want to be able to find the camp when it gets dark. And if anyone comes messing around, we'll know if they trip this string," he said as he softly plucked the twine.

The girls strapped their Zap-Guns across their hips. Jesse threw a small backpack with a folding shovel and a flashlight over his shoulder. Up the low edge of the cliffs the gang went. The ridge was filled with caves and caverns, Bess knew. They weren't as well known or as interesting as the Carlsbad Caverns down in the Chihuahuan Desert. Bess had gone down there a few years before to see the stalactites and stalagmites in the big rooms and caves. But there were caves in the mountains around Crescent Ridge. Anything could be hiding in them.

At the top of the ridge they found small holes in the mountainside. The holes were tiny, and went down into the mountain. They were way too small and steep to enter.

Bess stopped over the second one. "Do you smell that?" she sniffed.

Jesse leaned over the hole. "Pew! Holy cats, that smells like a gym locker room!"

"I'm not going down there!" interjected Lydia.

"I wonder what's making that smell?" thought Aurora out loud.

"Well, you can go find out," Bess said, "and then come back and tell us."

"No thank you!" Aurora held her nose and waved her hand at the stink.

They left the strange smell behind them as they hiked higher.

"What do you think caused that smell?" Aurora asked.

Bess thought about it, but then Lydia blurted out, "It could be trapped water, decaying plants ..."

"A skunk," Jesse chimed in.

Bess didn't say anything. She didn't know what it was. Jesse and Lydia were both right. It smelled rancid and soiled, but Jesse's comment about how it smelled like a locker room was closest. The scent had a vaguely human smell, of dirty socks and armpits and ... sweat.

"Look! Up there!" Bess pointed to a dark spot on the ridge. A shaded cave entrance was guarded by tufts of green weeds tangled around the entrance. "C'mon, we can get in there," she urged.

The four entered the cave. Bess and Lydia pulled out their Zap-Guns, turned the dials down, and lit the inside walls of the cave with a soft blue light. Jesse pulled his flashlight out and came in after the girls.

"You smell anything here?" asked Bess.

They all stopped. "Maybe, but not really. It's not as bad as those holes were, that's for sure. Kind of just smells like rock," said Aurora.

"Yeah," added Jesse, "I don't get much. Like dirt and moss, not like gym socks."

They kept walking. The cave would go from completely black to bare shafts of light, where cracks from far above would shine down on them.

"We must be heading into the mountain," said Jesse. He pulled a compass out of his backpack. "Yeah, south, maybe southeast."

Suddenly his compass needle spun and pointed east. The kids thought they heard and felt an almost imperceptible soft vibration coming through the rocks.

"What is that?" Aurora squeaked out. "Another earthquake?"

"No," Bess answered. "It's not an earthquake. Don't worry, look, nothing's moving, no trembling. It's a harmonic." Bess recognized the mechanical feeling right away. Something far off was vibrating at high speed, like a wheel that was a little off balance. "C'mon, let's see what's causing this."

Deeper into the cave they went. Bess felt her teeth and ears ache a little from the strange vibration. They were certainly getting closer. Bess put her hand on the cave wall. She could feel the vibration through the rock.

The cave opened wider, and the kids saw some light filter in through the darkness. Bess snapped her Zap-Gun off, and pushed Lydia's muzzle down until she turned hers off, too. To the back, Jesse snapped off his light.

They got closer to the fuzzy glare of light coming from somewhere inside the mountain. The humming was louder. Bess could feel it from her feet to her head. The group finally made a turn that led them to the end of the cave that opened to a great cavern full of light.

The light came from bright white bulbs suspended above the cavern floor hundreds of feet below. Machines, barrels, crates, and giant tools covered the far end. The humming rang loud through the cavern, then stopped with a slowing whine that ran down to a whimper. This only allowed all the other noises of machinery to be heard more clearly.

As the kids came closer to the edge of the cave opening, they could see farther down into the cavern. One side of the wall was rock, but it wavered like water. Bess rubbed her eyes. It was hard to focus on the wall. It was there, but not entirely.

The rock wall faded and waved, like a giant curtain in a breeze. A box truck drove right through the rock curtain as if it wasn't there. The truck was dark green, and the container was white, with a green stripe, but had been painted over to disguise it somewhat. Bess had seen the truck before but couldn't recognize it.

They walked to the cave exit, where a pile of rocks created a half wall for them to hide behind. Past the rocks were a series of ledges that spiraled down into the cavern. The ledges and paths were strewn with metal storage boxes and barrels. As they crept past the rocks, the kids could finally see fully down into the brightly lit cavern.

There they saw the men, about fifty of them, all clad in long cloaks and tight caps over their heads, as they worked intently to move barrels or unload the truck. It looked like they were hauling meat out of the container, all frozen and glistening with frost.

But that wasn't what scared the kids. Bess grabbed Aurora by the arm and squeezed. Lydia gasped silently, and Jesse breathed a soft exclamation, "... wow ..."

In the great cavern sat five round craft on tripod legs. They were smooth and rounded, and painted a mix of dull gray and flat green.

"Are those ..." Jesse could hardly bring himself to say the words, "... flying saucers?"

CHAPTER 10

A Crowbar In The Plans

Bess looked over the scene, trying to take in just what they saw. It was too much to believe. In the middle of the great cavern sat five flying saucers. They were all about fifty feet across, about the same size as the Starlighter, Bess estimated. But these were as different as can be to her aircraft.

The saucers were circular, with soft, blunt round edges and no sharp angles. If the Starlighter was a pie pan, these things were ... Bess tried to think of what they looked like. They looked like flying saucers, because that's what they were.

"What is happening?" Lydia said in a stunned whisper. "Are those ..." she struggled to find the words, "Martians or something?"

"I don't know," Bess commented. "What are they doing here is what I want to know." She looked down at all the machinery and supplies they were moving and storing.

"Look! Look!" Aurora pointed down at a section of the cavern as Bess grabbed her arm and pulled it down before they got noticed. "Sorry, but, look over there. See, they have these showers. Look at the pipes."

Bess looked where Aurora had pointed. Ten of the men below had gone into a sealed booth. Behind frosted plexiglass Bess could make out the men putting their cloaks into boxes before getting onto a conveyor belt that took them through a steaming shower. The steam was then sucked up through pipes with big boxes on them. The pipes separated to two sections, with one going to a huge wall of tubes and filters and the other going up into the roof of the cavern. "I bet that was the stench we smelled," Bess said. "But what ..." She was cut off by another loud whirring sound.

"It's that big round thing there," Lydia nodded toward the front wall. A huge round cylinder of thick metal was surrounded by giant coils, like some squat muscle man flexing his arms as they hung down to the ground. The machine must have been twelve feet tall.

Bess recognized the device, but couldn't believe what she saw. The wall of liquids running through filters made her sure of what it was.

"That's a cyclotron," she stated firmly. She knew it from the photos her mother showed her. "And that wall is a thermal diffusion unit." She looked around, and, hidden behind one of the saucers she saw part of a distinctive upside down U-shaped machine, a brutal looking tool that two of the strange looking men worked at with diligence and concern. "And, yup, that's a mass spectrometer."

"I don't know what you are saying. It's all Greek to me," said Aurora.

"Me, too," said Lydia. Jesse said nothing. He just waited for Bess to go on.

"They're making radioactive material," she said, quietly, gravely.

Everyone was silent after that. They knew the danger of radiation. Everyone had seen pictures of the explosions both near them at White Sands and farther away in Nevada. They knew that uranium and plutonium were used in making nuclear weapons.

"You think those guys are Russians?" Jesse asked.

Bess looked over the strange looking people in their strange looking clothes. All the men sweated under their robes and cloaks, even though it was cool in the cavern. They were all pale, with dark eyes. But they didn't look like Russians. There were no Soviet flags, no markings on the weird saucers. Bess looked closer at the saucers.

The center of them had a clear dome like the Starlighter. That must be the cockpit, Bess reasoned. But the rest of the saucer was a big dull round shell, except that a middle section, a ring around the cockpit, was open in one. She could see seats that ran in a circle around the saucer. "Twenty five seats," Bess counted. "Five ships."

"I need to get closer," Bess said. She needed to see more of what was going on down there. She still hadn't seen what could have blasted her out of the night sky. "C'mon, those lights all face down. They can't see up here even if they looked."

The four of them crept slowly from their hiding place, watching intently as the men below continued to work. No one noticed the kids as they worked their way down the inside of the cavern.

They walked slowly down the side of the cavern. Soon, they found boxes and crates stored along the walls. The boxes had funny writing on them, and the kids couldn't read any of it.

"You think it's, um, Russian, what is it?" Jesse asked.

"You mean Cyrillic?" Bess whispered. Cyrillic was the written form of the Russian language, along with other eastern European nations. "No, I don't think so. That still uses some recognizable letters. This looks completely different than any lettering I've ever seen." To Bess it was not quite a pictogram, but not any form of letters, either. It wasn't anything Asian, definitely not Mandarin or Cantonese, Korean, or Japanese, at least. She was tempted to open up a box just to see what the label was saying.

"Hey, look at that." Aurora had been moving down farther on the darkened path toward the well lit ground floor. She could see more of what had been under them and out of sight now. Two enormous continuous treads stuck out of a tall alcove on the floor of the cavern. They were like the treads of a tractor, but much bigger. They were easily eight feet tall. On top of them ran a large clear dome, the driving seat for the tracks, Aurora guessed.

The rest of the kids joined Aurora as they stared at the giant machine. Attached on top of the treads, standing two stories tall, was an enormous ray gun. It was painted flat black, dull and lifeless, but had a sharp crystalline end, and a single flash ring, similar to the end of the girls' Zap-Guns, only much, much bigger

"That must be the one that got me," Bess said in awe.

From somewhere in the middle of the cavern came a heated conversation. Bess couldn't recognize the words as they mingled with the strange sounds crashing through the cavern, but neither could someone else, as she heard a man's voice shout, "Speak English! You know I don't understand your language well." Bess thought the voice sounded familiar.

She wanted to hear what they were discussing. Something about the meat and food coming off the truck, she guessed. The truck looked so familiar, but she couldn't recognize it since parts of it had been hastily painted to cover it.

She started to sneak closer to the bottom of the cavern. She had to find out what they were saying. She scurried over to a tall set of boxes, followed by Aurora and Lydia. Jesse stopped when they heard strange voices and people walking nearby. All of them were silent as two cloaked men walked past the boxes the kids hid behind. The tall stack of boxes hid a room that was unlike the rest of the cave. It was obviously created by the strange men that hid in the cavern. The room was white and sterile. The walls were seamless and white, like it was carved out of ivory. It was the only place left for the girls to hide while the strange men walked around nearby. Bess went in.

Inside were more boxes, but this time they were open. They were all brushed metal, slightly polished and smooth. Steel tables held trays of vials laid out from the boxes. Aurora followed her in. "Bess, we have to be careful. Those weird guys could come in here any second."

"Gimme your M&Ms," Lydia walked in silently behind Aurora. Jesse was still hidden outside, and couldn't get to the room without being noticed.

"This is no time for a snack," said Aurora, clutching at her pocket.

"Just gimme," insisted Lydia. She snatched the bag from Aurora and tore open the top. She went back to the entrance and began scattering the little tan peanut M&Ms all over the entrance. "Now we will hear them coming, at least."

"Look at these things," Bess picked up the little vials. They were filled with clear pills. The capsules were transparent, and inside were tiny white pellets. There must have been thousands of them. Along with the pills were small backpacks with tubes on them. Lydia picked one up. It sloshed.

"Water? Strange way to make a canteen," Lydia said. She flipped the backpack over in her hands. "Why do they need so many?"

Bess took one of the tubes in her hand, squeezed the end, and had some of the water pour out. She sipped some from her hand.

"Don't do that! You don't know what it is!" Aurora said. "We need to get out of here."

"For once, I agree," said Lydia.

"Yeah, you're right," Bess agreed. "Let's get back to camp and get back to town and tell my folks what's going on. Maybe those G-Men are still in town." She took one of the vials and put it in her pocket.

Just then, they heard a crunch. The girls froze as they heard a voice make some guttural sound. Bess signaled to hide. The room had only one door, and one of the strange men was coming in. They ducked behind the two end tables. It was the only place left to hide.

Bess pulled her Zap-Gun. She never used it on a person before. It would hurt, but it may not stop a person. It may just make him mad.

The man stopped inside the room. Bess could see his shadow, vaguely, as he stood only a few feet away. They heard him make some noise, "Aaarctch... Cuurrr..." and he scraped his foot on the floor.

The side of the tables were thin steel sheets. Lydia and Aurora were crowded around one table while Bess hid behind another. Lydia pressed up against the steel, and it made a soft deep *pong* as the metal compressed.

It got very quiet for a moment. Then the shadow started moving toward Bess and her friends. There was nowhere to hide and nowhere to go. Bess had no choice left. She pushed off the back of the table and slid across the smooth floor. She spun around, pointing her Zap-Gun at the towering hulking shadow of the man in the cloak. She saw him clearly for a fraction of a second. His eyes were surrounded by black circles, and his skin was sallow and ghostly pale. His eyes widened for the moment he saw Bess pointing her Zap-Gun at him. His thin dark lips opened in a moment of surprise. He loomed over the girl on the floor, a giant in black and white.

Then another shadow loomed up behind him. Now two giants towered over Bess.

CLANG!

CHAPTER 11

Escape!

The big man froze, as if he was struck by the discovery of the girls. Then he crumpled and fell to the floor. Behind him, the other towering shadow stepped forward.

Jesse grinned as he held his unfolded shovel aloft. He had followed the man in and conked him on the head with it.

"Who's your favorite crowbar?" he asked.

Bess jumped up. "Jesse!" Aurora almost screamed before she covered her mouth.

Jesse pulled Lydia up with a helping hand. "C'mon, guys, we gotta beat sneakers out of here before this fella gets up. He's got a hard head."

"More like a hard helmet," Bess said as she looked at the man. He was unconscious, but he wore a tight skull cap helmet over his head that protected him somewhat from the blow. "Look at him. He's so pale, and sweaty."

Aurora backed away, toward the door. "I don't care, let's go, Jesse's right." She waved the rest of them toward the exit.

"Hang on," Bess grabbed metal strapping ribbon from one of the open boxes. She wrapped it around the man's hands. Then she set the dial on her Zap-Gun and pointed at the twisted metal. With a quick *snap* the thin metal fused together into makeshift handcuffs. They dragged the unconscious man behind some boxes to hide him. "It won't keep him for long, but hopefully long enough for us to escape," Bess said hopefully.

"Let's go," Jesse hissed from the door. The four took off into the shadows at a low run. Almost immediately there were shouts and strange commands coming from the floor behind them as they worked their way up the path of the cavern wall. They froze, hidden behind some empty barrels. "They couldn't have discovered us yet," Aurora insisted.

Bess looked over the barrel. Men scattered toward the rock curtain and carved out pathways at the bottom of the cavern. "They haven't. Something else happened." She heard someone shouting in English, and the voice sounded familiar. As she strained to listen and see who it was, Lydia pulled her arm.

"Quick, while they are distracted!"

Jesse led the other four up the cavern to the cave where they came in. Once clear of the opening, he switched on his flashlight. Bess was right behind him with her Zap-Gun on. They made their way out much more quickly than when

84

they came in. They came out to the opening in the mountain with a rush into the open air.

It was a significant change from the cool, humid, and bright cavern. The sun had set, and the sky had turned to a clear dark purple, with stars shining in the sky. A sliver of a quarter moon hung like a white sickle in the sky. The air was warm and incredibly dry. The kids breathed in the familiar air deeply.

They worked their way down almost silently, with only soft warnings, "watch your step," "loose rock," "careful," to break the silence. They were able to get down the low mountainside quickly. They moved quietly toward the river. Jesse looked for the lamp he hung over the camp. The red light would be hard to find until they got close, but they would notice it when they were nearby.

It took a few minutes to find the right path back to the camp. The four of them got within one hundred feet when they could see the dull glow of the red light. "There it is," Jesse whispered.

Bess grabbed the back of Jesse's shirt. She said nothing, which made the rest of them stop. Bess had seen something moving in the darkness. A shape moved along the edge of the camp. As it came closer to the light, Bess could make out a human form. It moved around the camp until it tripped over Jesse's string and the lamp began to wobble. Whoever it was tried to get up and grab the lamp.

Bess took off at a run straight into the camp, with her Zap-Gun pulled. As she stormed in, the figure spun around.

Bess saw it was a man, and his arm turned toward her, holding a short barreled weapon in his hand. Bess pointed her Zap-Gun and fired.

CHAPTER 12

Welcome To Three Winds

"AAAAAHHHH!" the man screamed as the weapon fell from his hand. He fell to his knees and held his arm where the powerful static bolt had gone up his wrist from the metal of the strange weapon he held.

Bess ran forward before the man had a chance to get up. Jesse and Aurora followed her, while Lydia kicked the weapon into the shadow covered sand.

"Joel?!" Bess was stunned. On his knees in the campsite was her ranch foreman, looking up at her in pain and fear. More fear, Bess noticed. Of course he would be afraid, Bess thought, he's finally been caught after his sabotage.

"Bess?!" Joel actually seemed to relax. His body sighed as he let out a deep breath. "Thank goodness... wait, what are you doing out here?" he stammered.

This wasn't going how Bess thought it would. He didn't seem like a saboteur caught in the act. He seemed happy to be caught. "That's what I was going to ask you, Joel.

You ran off after sabotaging the Starlighter. You made us crash and almost killed us. Are you in league with those, those, people in the mountain? Who are they? Russians?"

"What? Sabotage?!" Joel was stunned at the accusation. He blubbered in fear. "No. It wasn't me, honestly.

"It was Kenneth."

Bess lowered her Zap-Gun. She realized now who it was she heard speaking in the cavern. Kenneth, their weekend foreman.

"I caught him sneaking around the hangar, and he slugged me and brought me here."

"But why?" Bess couldn't imagine a reason Kenneth would turn on her family. "Is he working with those Russians?"

"Russians?" Joel was perplexed. "Bess," Joel slowly got up, rubbing his wrist, "those aren't Russians. They are from the moon."

"What?!" Aurora almost yelled it out.

"Moon men?!" Lydia gasped. "You mean, like an invasion from outer space or something?"

Joel shook his head. Bess saw a bruise and cut on his jaw, and his eyes were sunken and red. He didn't look well. "An invasion? No. You don't understand.

"They're already here."

They helped Joel into Jesse's car. "We need to get home and let Mom and Dad know what's going on," Bess ordered. Joel leaned forward in the seat and held his head. "I'm sorry I hurt you, Joel. I didn't know who you were. I thought you were one of those," it was hard for Bess to contemplate it, "moon men."

"My arm's alright. It's tingling, but it's there," Joel answered. "No, it's my head. There's something you gotta know about those moon men."

Jesse started up his buggy and floored it. "Just relax, pal," Jesse said with confidence. "We'll get you out of here and to a doctor."

"No, listen, it's more than that," Joel was insistent. The car ride shook him, and Bess could tell he was uncomfortable. "Those moon men, they are, they're sick, see ..." he tried to explain. "They fouled up the moon where they live. It's radioactive now. And so are they."

Jesse slowed for a moment to listen, then he stomped the gas pedal down. No playing around in the desert this time. He had to move.

Bess asked, "Are you sick? You have radiation poisoning? Is that why you feel bad?"

"I don't know." Joel pulled out a thin tube he had in an inside pocket to his pants. "They never bothered to search me. I still got this. If we can get this to your mother, we can see how bad it is. I may just be sick.

"Or I may be a dead man."

Joel held out a dosimeter. It was a small tube that measured how much radiation a person has been exposed to. With the uranium mine, even though they took every precaution, Bess's mother insisted on dosimeters and regular checks.

Bess took it and tried to look through the tube, but the car bounced around too much, and it was too dark to see inside.

"Are you nauseous? You feel sick to your stomach?"

"No, just a headache. They didn't get too close to me when they had me. When I felt my first headache a couple hours ago, I knew I had to get out. I escaped and found your camp. I was just hoping to find someone to take me back to town."

"How do they survive it?"

Joel shrugged. "They take some pills, and then they sweat it out. All of them were sweaty and filthy. They take like a pill every hour."

"Like these?" Bess handed the vial she took to Joel. It was hard to see in the dark.

"Yes," he exclaimed. He looked at Bess, who looked back and shrugged. If Joel had only received a little radiation, he would likely survive. But too much radiation and he was definitely dead.

Joel cracked the top and took a pill. "Got any water?"

The car made it to the main road, and Jesse opened it up to full speed. His headlights burned out onto the shiny asphalt. If any animal ran out in front of him, well, bad luck for all of them. "Not like we've had any good luck so far," Jesse thought, as his left foot lifted to hover over his brake petal, just in case. But he didn't slow down.

"Can you tell me about Kenneth?" Bess asked. Joel seemed better just by drinking some water and thinking about the medicine he took.

"Kenneth, that guy's a monster," Joel commented like he had battery acid in his mouth. "He's working with those moon men. They're creating a base so they can take over the atomic lab at Los Alamos and Holloman Air Force Base, then attack the West Coast. They're trying to take over and bring the rest of the people down from the moon."

Now everyone in the car felt sick. They sat with their stomachs heavy with the threat on their home, and how much worse it all was than they realized.

"But why? Why would he do that?"

"Why else? Money, power, greed. He's in cahoots with James Fields," Joel pointed over to a sprawling ranch to the north of Three Winds.

Bess snapped her fingers. "Fields Meat Packing! That's where I recognized that truck!" The green and white truck was the color of the meat packing company run by James Fields. He was the Trulys' biggest competitor in the region. He had tried to take over and run Bess's family out of town, as well as anyone else who tried to do something in Three Winds that he couldn't control. "Kenneth used to work for him. He's probably been planning this since he got hired."

"I'm not sure how he got mixed up in it. I just know they are planning to use this area as a staging point."

"We've got to get home, Jesse. We need to get help before they find out where you are," Bess was insistent.

"We might have a problem with that," Jesse said as he adjusted his rear view mirror.

Everyone else looked over their shoulders. In the darkness, an eerie green glow appeared over the ridge they had escaped from only minutes earlier. A blunt round saucer rose up in the vivid green light. It wobbled in the night air before starting to move forward.

"If they find us ..." Bess started ominously. No one needed her to finish the sentence.

"Maybe they can't find us in the dark," suggested Aurora.

Jesse switched off his headlights. For a terrifying second, the road got dark as midnight, before their eyes got accustomed to the night and the thin moonlight that helped illuminate the road. Jesse slowed his car slightly. The flying saucer wandered through the air. It didn't move in one direction, and had a hard time moving in the changing winds coming from the plains and mountainside.

"I don't think they saw us," Aurora said.

"We're not going to be able to hide from them for long." Jesse pointed forward.

They were only a few miles from town. The road, straight and flat, was lit at night by light poles at regular intervals. About a mile away was a huge well lit billboard that read "Welcome To Three Winds NM."

Jesse turned on his headlights and floored his accelerator. The old Ford roared as he sped up.

And the flying saucer turned toward them.

CHAPTER 13

Breaking The Genie's Bottle

"We're not going to make it back to town." Bess was sure of that. The moon saucer was definitely moving toward them now that Jesse's orange dune buggy was in the lights of the road. It still wobbled in the air, but it was steadily catching up with them. "Let me out behind the sign."

"Are you crazy? You can't stop that on your own!" Aurora yelled over the wind in the car, and over her own fears.

"You need to get Joel back home. He needs medical help. And we need to tell someone what's happening. We're going to have to get the Army or the Air Force in here. I'll slow it down or distract it."

They were getting closer to the sign. The saucer was even closer to them.

"We don't have any choice!" Bess yelled.

Aurora picked up the strange weapon Joel had taken from the moon men. "Can we use this on them?" she asked.

"Whoa!" Joel grabbed the steel pistol from Aurora. It was short with an egg-shaped barrel and thick handle. "Let me have that. I saw one of these things blast a boulder bigger than this car out of the mountain. I think they use some sort of atomic discharge. But it's a one shot thing, and it takes forever to reload."

"We need to get that to Mom," Bess said. "We need to know how it works. Which means I've got to stop that flying saucer." She looked insistently at Jesse, who kept his head facing the road, but his eyes darted back and forth between the upcoming sign and Bess.

"Well? Anyone gonna talk her out of this?" he said.

No one spoke. Jesse waited until they were as close as possible and slammed on the brakes. The car skidded with a high pitched whine as all of them were pushed forward in their seats. Bess jumped out and began to run behind the sign, into the dark shadow made by the giant board and its lights. Jesse stomped his car back up to speed like a dragster, wheels smoking to get a grip on the pavement. Bess saw him take off, and as the smoke cleared, she saw Lydia run to the other side of the road.

"You didn't think I was going to miss out on the fun, did you?" she grinned as she pulled out her Zap-Gun.

Bess did the same. She dialed the Zap-Gun up, then, with a decidedly ominous *click*, she locked in the highest setting. On the other side of the road, she heard Lydia's Zap-Gun make the same distinctive *click*.

The orange jalopy roared off into the distance, closing in on the town. Every second Bess could save meant that they could be closer to the relative safety of the buildings and people. As soon as the sound of Jesse's car disappeared, Bess heard the ominous hum of the flying saucer.

She glanced out from behind the sign. The flying saucer was spinning toward her, its strange engine propelling it across the barren prairie and empty road. "I'm going to get it to turn," Bess said to Lydia. "When it goes this way, you hit its engine from the back." Then she stepped out into the road.

Bess waited only a second for the flying saucer to get close. She didn't want to miss, and even if the thing was huge and coming right at her, it was still a moving target bouncing through the air. Bess could see the look on the moon man's face that piloted the saucer. It was one of surprise, and then anger. He worked hidden controls to slew the saucer, but it wasn't working well in the air. Bess fired a blue blast straight at the ship.

A lightning bolt erupted from the tip of her Zap-Gun. It crackled across the distance to the saucer, which seemed to race straight into the bright static charge. The light ripped across the front of the flying saucer, pulling paint and metal with it. The middle ring of seats was empty of moon men, which was a good thing, as the clear canopy crackled and shattered where the Zap-Gun's ray moved across it.

The blue bolt snapped with electricity as it worked its way up the saucer and onto the cockpit canopy. The clear glass cracked, then splintered and turned milky white, but didn't break. Bess held the trigger down while the bolt continued to pour out of her Zap-Gun. It clung to the top of the saucer canopy, emitting sparks into the night like an otherworldly Tesla coil.

Bess let go of the trigger and moved immediately to hide behind the sign. The saucer dipped and made a painful whine. Something had been damaged inside, Bess knew. Then it stopped and began to lift. From the underside she saw a smaller version of the giant ray gun extend from the saucer. Bess could see a green glow coming brightly from the inside of the ship. She tried to run back up to the road and into the darkness of the other side, but the dry road bed and gravel gave her little traction. The saucer's gun would fire any moment.

At that second, another blue flash came from the darkness on the opposite side of the road. Lydia came from her hiding place pouring out blue lightning into the saucer's underside.

The ship began to flip backwards from the impact of Lydia's blast, and the ray gun discharged its explosive green beam into the big welcome sign. It splintered to bits, raining paper and wood down around Bess as she ran away with her arms over her head to protect herself from debris.

The saucer was flying backwards now. The ray gun discharge and the attack had made it unstable in the air. "It must not be able to handle well in the atmosphere," thought Bess. She put away the thought for the present. Raising her

Zap-Gun, she let loose with another blue blast into the ducts that must control the saucer's flight. She was rewarded with a loud clank and a huge chunk of metal falling off onto the road. The ship began to spin. It looked off balance now with one of its engines out of commission. Lydia took off toward it as the saucer tumbled out toward the prairie. She pointed as she ran, shooting blue lightning that skidded across the metal. She got the satisfaction of a loud pop and a cloud of smoke.

The saucer was going down. It stood little chance after the onslaught that Bess and Lydia poured into it. The girls stopped and watched as the ship tumbled sideways, then buried itself into the sand. There was a violent clanking sound, repeated over and over, until that, too, finally gave up with a resigned whimper.

Bess and Lydia looked at each other, then began running toward the ship. Bess wanted to make sure it wasn't going to rise back up. Lydia followed Bess to see what would happen next.

When they got there, they could see in the relative darkness the ship, crashed and bent in the ground. There was just enough light from the streetlamps to see the ship smoking. A hatch opened next to the cockpit and the moon man pilot crawled out. He limped down the cracked hull of the ship and jumped into the sand.

Bess and Lydia ran up to him, Bess dialing her Zap-Gun down to light up the man in blue light. It did nothing more than make him shield his eyes, but the threat was there. He began to fumble with something on his belt.

"Nope!" Lydia yelled from the darkness, as she fired a quick zap into the dirt near the man. His hands went up and out to the sides. Bess assumed it was the moon man's version of surrender.

"What will you do, Earth people?" he said in a sneer. "You can't get near me. I can kill you without any weapon."

"You speak English?" Bess said from the darkness.

"Yes, I speak English, certainly.

"Ya govoryu po-russki.

"Wǒ shuō pǔtōnghuà.

"Je parle français.

"Watashi wa nihongo o hanashimasu."

Bess recognized some of the languages, but not all.

"I speak all of your languages. We need to communicate with you well. In order for you to follow our orders."

"I don't think I'm going to be taking any orders from you. I got your space ship down, didn't I?" Bess wasn't going to let this moon man try to get out of this.

"Earth girl, you know you cannot stop me. I will make you sick if you get near me. You have little choice. Now, back away or regret the consequences."

"Yeah?" Lydia chimed in, "Or what?"

"We have more than one ship," the moon man sneered. Over his shoulder, a green light appeared over the mountain range. Another ship lifted over the cliffs and began its slow wobble toward town.

"You don't fly so well in our atmosphere, I guess," Bess said. She wanted to see if the proud moon man would give up any information. She didn't wait long.

"Atmosphere? We fly using your gravity, powered by your own uranium. We must adjust our ships to your gravity and then nothing will stop them," he said. The moon man watched the saucer as it got closer and closer. It continued to follow the road. It didn't turn to the wrecked ship. Bess wasn't sure if they were afraid of being attacked, or if they just didn't care.

"They don't seem to be coming to save you," Bess commented.

"No," said the moon man. "They have another job."

As if on cue, the ship stopped at the street lights, above a tall power line leading into the town. A soft puff of luminescent green flew out from the back of the saucer's hull. It looked like a shooting star, Bess thought, as it flew through the night sky. It went up and up. Bess could barely make out a small shape, like a little winged glider, with tiny pulses of green energy coming out the back. She half heard, half imagined, a raspy whistle as the glider rocket flew through the air. It disappeared into the night over the center of Three Winds. Then there was a soft pop where the missile went, and a sprinkling of the green energy dissipated in the air.

Nothing happened for a moment. Then Bess saw the flying saucer drop a shining chrome ball out the bottom of the ship. It flopped on a wire from the ship and almost touched the power line.In a fit of sparks, it sent a bright charge of electricity down the line, straight into the town.

All the lights in Three Winds went out for a second time.

This time the lights stayed off.

"I think I need to be going," said the moon man, as he limped off into the darkness. He was right. There was no way to stop him.

He slowly moved off to the north.

The only lights still on were coming from that direction. The entire Fields cattle ranch was lit up with green light.

Bess and Lydia started running to town as fast as they could.

CHAPTER 14

Fire On Approach!

It had taken almost an hour for Bess and Lydia to run all the way back through town and then to the ranch. By the time they had made it into the darkened streets, some of the homes in town began to light up with the soft glow of candles and oil lamps. Shadows passed over windows with soft curtains still drawn. Most of the people in town were asleep, and many wouldn't know what had happened just outside their town.

Bess didn't want to stop to warn them. She needed to get home. They stopped only for a moment to try to call her house, but the phone lines were dead. "That rocket took out the power and the phone," Bess noticed. She looked out over the town. Even the red blinking light on the radio tower was off. She could barely see the dark scaffold of the antenna in the night sky.

"I need to get home and tell my folks what's going on," Lydia told Bess. "If they'll even believe me."

"Tell them to look outside," Bess muttered grimly.

They separated, and Bess began the long run to her house. About a mile from her ranch she found Jesse's dune buggy. It sat blank and lifeless in the road. The car must have been turned off, too, by the strange rocket blast.

By the time she made it back to the C Bar M, the ranch and airstrip was lit up, both with oil lamps, and with flashlights. The hum of generators came steadily from many of the buildings. The C Bar M had power. And manpower, Bess noticed.

Everyone was up. Two of the cowboys that rode the line spotted her. They clopped up the long drive on their horses to take Bess back to the ranch house. Inside, her parents gushed over her. They were overjoyed to get her home. Her father held her close and looked her over. "No ray gun scars from those moon goons," he said. She filled them in on bringing down the moon saucer and her encounter with the moon man.

"That fits with what Joel told us," Portia said.

"Oh, goodness! Yes, Joel... Mom, he wasn't the saboteur. It was..."

"Yes, Joel told us," Portia cut her off. "I knew it wasn't him. Joel has been with us too long and could be trusted. Plus, why would he leave such a blatant clue like his knife behind. I was surprised to learn about Kenneth, though."

"How is he? Joel seemed like he was very sick," Bess worried the person who exposed the invasion from the moon would not live to see how he warned the town.

"He'll be fine," Portia assured Bess. "He only received about 70 Rads. That pill you gave him is a rather curious medicine. It seems to be a chelator. It pulls the radiation from his body."

"That must be why the moon men sweat so much," Bess said. "They must be removing their radiation with the pills through their body."

Bess's mother took the information in without comment. It was important, but not important right now.

"Why are all the lights out?" Bess asked.

"Because of the EMP," came a voice from outside her father's office. Bess turned to see the Chair come in. Agent Marsh, she corrected herself.

"What's an EMP?" asked Steve.

Agent Marsh entered the room, followed by Agent Phillips. "An electromagnetic pulse. They happen during nuclear explosions," he explained.

"But that was no atomic bomb I saw," Bess stated. "There was barely an explosion."

"Yes, that is true," Agent Marsh went on. "We think it was a chemical, or non-nuclear EMP," he said coolly.

He was talking way over Bess's head, but her mother seemed to nod in agreement. "Yes, likely, only because there seems to be no other explanation. You seem to know a lot about this, for a," she paused for emphasis, "G-Man." She finished with her daughter's slang for the FBI agent.

"But you're not really an FBI agent, are you, Mr. Marsh?" Portia went on.

Marsh took off his hat, revealing his black close cropped hair. "No ma'am. I should have known you would figure that out."

Steve Truly turned to the man, "So, who are you then? Who do you work for?"

"Same people you do, Mr. Truly. Or, Major Truly," Marsh used Steve's former Army Air Corps title. "America. The free world. And right now, all of Earth it may seem."

The room got small all of a sudden. There were five people in the room that had the whole picture. They all knew this was the beginning of an invasion. The invasion that had already started, Bess realized. She remembered Joel's words, "They're already here."

"What are we going to do? Joel brought back one of their pistols. If it's anything like that ray gun on the saucer, or the big one they have at the Crater, we are going to have a hard time standing up to that onslaught." She cringed at the explosion of the sign so close to her not more than an hour ago. "Can we use that weapon against them?"

Portia paced the small room, parting the little crowd as she moved. "I looked at that device. Yes, it is extremely powerful, but it only has one shot before reloading. It seems to be powered by atomics. There is an insert that contains a radioactive catalyst, only a small number of atoms, I can only guess, but they create a pre-nuclear reaction that makes a powerful blast. The barrel seems to be some sort of miniature electromagnet that directs the charge. I would like to see the moon people's blood. I'd be amazed if all their iron isn't sucked out through the skin with one of those. I would bet that in addition to being sick with radiation, they are also anemic." She stopped her pacing to consider all the ramifications. "But that's not important now. We cannot duplicate the weapon, nor can we provide the ammunition. They seem to be diabolical in the time it takes to reload, from what Joel expressed. We may do better with capable tactics and our current weaponry." She patted her hip where her Zap-Gun hung in its holster. "Bess and one other girl brought down one of their ships with only two of these. I feel that if the rest of the Zap-Gun Rangers were involved, the moon men would stand little chance." Portia beamed at her daughter. She didn't really wish Bess would go into the fray of battling moon men, but she had all the faith and confidence that Bess would come out of any action better than her adversary.

"Well," sighed Marsh, "we may be able to help a little with that. I don't know about providing more weapons, but fortunately our airplane is hardened against attacks like this, and we were able to put a call through to some people who can help."

"The Army?" Bess asked.

"Something like that," Marsh answered cryptically.

At that moment, J.C., one of the ranch hands, burst into the house, clopping on the wooden floor of the entryway with his cowboy boots.

"Sir, ahh…" he looked around, surprised to see the room full of people. He found Steve Truly's face.

"What is it, J.C.?"

"Those space ship things appeared, sir. They're moving."

The whole group jumped up and ran outside. From far off, dull green glows appeared over the ridge. There was little to see except the light they cast.

"Are they coming this way?" Bess asked.

J.C. handed Steve binoculars that hung around his neck. "I don't know, sir. I was watching like you said, and they just appeared."

Steve looked through the binoculars. "No, they are moving to the north side of town." He bit his tongue and spat, "They're going to James Fields' ranch. How could he sell out his town, everyone, his nation, like that?"

"Greed. Power." Marsh commented. "Look at any event where someone wishes destruction on another. Hate. Power over others. The ability to hurt. The inability to care. Selfishness. You've seen it before," he directed his comments with a nod to Steve. "And, I would hazard a guess," he spoke to Portia, "so have you."

Bess only vaguely understood what Marsh was saying. She knew both her parents had fought in their own ways during World War II. They told her some of their stories, but never got too much into the 'why' questions she started to have. She thought that Marsh might have been hinting at some answers.

A figure came running up to the group. Bess didn't recognize him at first. Then she realized he was the pilot of the Bonanza.

"Agent Phillips," he said quietly, "we have incoming, sir."

"Thank you, Lieutenant," Agent Phillips said. Then he turned to Steve. "Can we get any lights on the airstrip, Mr. Truly? We have cavalry coming in."

Steve understood the meaning. There was a plane coming in loaded with soldiers, and they needed to see the landing field.

"We can do flashlights, flares, maybe some headlights, if they still work. We'll get the field lit for your boys," he insisted.

Steve gave orders to J.C., who ran off. Bess watched as Marsh went back to the house. A moment later, Jesse came running out with Marsh behind him. "Hey, Bess!" he yelled, running up and hugging his friend. "I knew those moon men wouldn't stand a chance with you!"

Aurora came out next, letting out a squeal as she saw Bess out in the soft light that filtered through the night. She grabbed Bess and swung her around. "I'm so glad you're alright," she yelled.

"Hey, Secret Agent Super Guy here told me we can get the cars working again if we just rewire the batteries, probably. I'm going to help get some of your trucks out on the tarmac, then go get the desert Cadillac. It conked out on your road. We had to beat feet to your place."

Bess wished Jesse luck. She went back to stand by the house with her family and Aurora. They looked at the skies to see if they could spot the plane in the darkness.

Five minutes later a huge effort had been made to light up the airstrip. Cars were restarted, generators pounded out electricity to lights, and red flares burned on the edge of the landing strip.

Then they heard it. Bess noticed it first, then a second later, everyone turned to the east. There was a low throbbing rumble coming out of the darkness.

They finally spotted the shape of the airplane as it cruised toward them. Even in the darkness, with the light of a crescent moon, Bess could see the shiny chrome of the big transport plane. Steve, ever the pilot, said, "Globemaster II." The big transport plane had low mounted wings with four engines on them. It was two stories tall and made to carry both heavy equipment and troops.

The plane came in low over the airport. The pilot dipped his wings to get a look at the runway, then circled around to make his approach from the east, so he would land into the wind. The plane had to increase altitude to make a better approach. Bess watched as it turned nearly sideways to make the long bank turn around the ranch. Then it lined up with the airstrip. It had to be high up for the huge plane to make its approach.

She was looking to the east, wondering if the saucers would see the plane, when she saw a glow come from far off by the Crater and Crescent Ridge. The green light flashed.

Bess remembered the same flash of green light when the Starlighter got knocked from the sky. There was nothing for her to do but watch.

A bolt of green energy struck the plane. One of the starboard engines crackled, smoked, and burst into flames. The whole plane bounced and then dipped from the explosion. It quickly fell in altitude as the engine, then the wing, began to burn.

The flames lit up the night sky as the huge airplane came hurtling toward the ranch.

CHAPTER 15

The Cavalry Arrives

The huge Globemaster roared over the ranch house trailing fire. For a moment, it looked like the big plane would land on its extended landing gear. The airplane came down hard, with a lurch, and crashed into the tarmac. Sparks flew as the belly of the plane scraped down the runway.

Bess watched, her feet frozen in place. The big plane crushed itself under its own weight. The propellers chopped into the airstrip before breaking apart. Even with all the destruction, the plane kept moving. It took a second for Bess to even notice the silhouettes of people running toward the burning plane. She forced her feet to get unglued and started running, too.

The plane finally stopped skidding by plowing into the sandy ground beside the airstrip. By the time Bess had gotten to the plane, the small fire truck they used at the airport was already spraying down the burning engine.

Bess feared the worst. The whole bottom of the big plane was crushed and flattened. The giant two wheeled landing gear lay broken and torn on the tarmac. She was sure no one could survive that kind of crash.

The underside of the craft had split open. Inside there were crushed Jeeps, mortars, and crates that split open spilling weapons and ammunition. Bess didn't see any soldiers.

Her father was up on the bent wing, opening a door near the port engine. It finally opened with a pop. Steve lost his balance and fell back onto the wing. Soldiers began spilling out of the plane and organizing themselves on the tarmac. Bess ran up to her father and helped him up.

"Looks like the cargo section took the big hit. I hope the boys are alright," he said with a wince of pain. The plane was made to open at the front and back to load vehicles and gear. It was so tall it had a second deck to handle troops as well. They had been cushioned from the heavy crash. Bess turned her Zap-Gun on to light up the wing so the men could see to get down. Soon the tarmac was filling up with camouflaged soldiers.

A big soldier jumped down on the wing with a dull thunk. Bess looked at the man, who noticed her Zap-Gun, but spoke to her father.

"Any landing you can walk away from," he said with a serious grimace. "I'm Captain Brooks." He put out his hand, but Steve didn't take it. "Who is in charge of this airstrip?"

Steve tried to lift his arm. "I guess I am, Cap," said Steve.

"Are you injured, sir?" the captain was concerned, but he didn't seem to want to waste time on a civilian.

"I think I got a busted wing, but nothing that won't heal. How are your boys?"

Captain Brooks looked at Steve again, and recognized the air of a fellow military officer. "Air Corps?" Captain Brooks guessed.

"Fighter pilot," Steve said.

"I need to get my men in a lit place, and salvage what we can out of the plane. Anything you can do to help."

"I'm on it. Bess, take the captain down, get Manny to open up Hangar One, and see if Jesse can get anything moving, we need trucks here."

"I want to go see if the crew needs help."

"Okay, dad," Bess said. Her father gingerly pulled himself into the plane to go check on the pilot and crew. The nose of the plane took a big part of the impact.

As Bess led the captain down, the soldiers were already forming lines to unload what equipment they could from the plane's cargo. "Top!" bellowed Captain Brooks. A sergeant ran up when he was called. "Sir, most of the men are functional. My corporal took a heavy hit and has a messed up back. We've got a broken arm and some cuts and bruises, Sir. We are probably at 95%. But the vehicles are a total loss, and sorting the weapons is going to take time."

"Personal weapons first, then tacticals," ordered the captain. He turned to Bess. "So this is your ranch? I guess you are in charge here, then." For a moment, he squinted and smiled at her. "We need a place for the men to be treated for injuries, get our gear untangled from this mess, and then we will need transportation. This is a lot for a girl to handle, but..."

"Manny!" Bess screamed. She did her best impression of the captain. Bess held up her Zap-Gun and flashed a bright blue signal in the air. Manny came running up. "Manny, listen, get Hangar One open, get it lit up, then find Asta, Sammy, anyone from the stables around here, and get them to me."

"Yes, ma'am, Miss Truly," said Manny, and he took off. "A lot for a girl," thought Bess. Of the two of them, she shot down a flying saucer and he crashed his own airplane.

The air strip ground crew had feverishly worked to quickly get the fire on the plane completely out. It took longer to rescue the soldiers inside and set up a small treatment area for the injured. Most of the soldiers flying in the hold were unhurt except for some bruises. There were a couple of concussions, a strained back, and a broken arm in the list of casualties. The airplane crew were not as fortunate. The rough landing had sent the cockpit slamming forward into the runway. Half of the six crew members had broken ribs. The load specialist that was supposed to get the supplies off the plane had been thrown around and had twisted his leg badly enough that he couldn't walk. A medic had given him medication for the pain and had wrapped the leg in a makeshift cast, but he would need a hospital to repair the damages he received. The rest of the crew suffered broken bones and gashes from the crash. Even Steve Truly had his arm wrapped up in a sling. He had injured it forcing open the emergency door.

Inside the hangar, the soldiers prepared their weapons. The sergeant reported to Captain Brooks, "Just like I thought, Sir, no transport survived the crash. The locals say some weapon took out all electronics, including cars, but they are rewiring some of them as we speak. Only a couple work trucks, Jeeps, and a civilian car so far."

Captain Brooks looked grim. This wasn't turning out the way he wanted, but plans never do as soon as the reality of battle hits them. He just wanted to hit back.

Agent Marsh found the captain and greeted him. "Alan," he said simply.

"Marsh," answered Captain Brooks, equally simply, but then the captain gave Agent Marsh a small smile. The two knew each other. "Well, looks like we're going to do this on foot. Any chance of local help? Police, fire? Anything?"

Agent Marsh called Bess over. "I don't know if there's much help on transportation, but if you need a guide to lead you, you'll be hard pressed to find anyone better than Bess Truly here."

"The girl?" Captain Brooks grimaced. He didn't like working with civilians, and teenage girls weren't his idea of soldiers. "I can't endanger the locals like that."

Marsh never changed his quiet tone. "If it weren't for Bess, we wouldn't know where the moon men were, what their plan is, how many ships they have. We wouldn't have one of their weapons intact, and one of their saucers crashed in the desert. I'd say you could do a lot worse, but really," he looked at Bess, "you couldn't do any better."

Bess smiled a look of satisfaction. She didn't like people doubting her before she even had a chance to prove herself. At least Agent Marsh seemed in her corner.

"And I can help with transportation, too," Bess added. She looked over her shoulder outside the hangar. When she saw what she was looking for, Bess stuck her fingers in her mouth and whistled loudly while waving. She looked back at Captain Brooks. "Can any of your men ride, Captain?"

Manny and his cowboys led a long string of saddled horses into the hangar.

CHAPTER 16

Battle Of Fields Ranch

An hour had passed and it was well after midnight by the time the soldiers had organized themselves into groups on horseback or in the few vehicles they had been able to restart. The fact that the plane had been spotted and then shot down was the biggest concern to Captain Brooks. It meant the moon men knew they were there, and knew they were coming.

"I wish we had some air cover, at least," complained Brooks. "I'd like to see what we're up against, and keep those flying saucers away if we could."

He asked one of his officers, "How many have you seen moving toward that ranch?"

"Counting the one the kid saw," the lieutenant jerked a thumb over at Bess, "we've had three go over there, and then one went back over the mountains."

Brooks turned to Bess, "And you say they hold twenty five people each? And the one you shot down was empty? Right?"

Bess answered, "Not counting the pilot, yes."

"So," Brooks sighed. "We have to take out the saucers, capture the enemy, cut off their means of escape and evasion, take over the base, and remove the threat of the ray gun. All while we can't get too near them, and they know we're coming, and we're losing night." He waved his hand vaguely into the darkness.

"Any chance that saucer of yours," Brooks started to speak to Steve Truly, who was wincing in pain as Portia adjusted his arm in a sling and tried to shove aspirin in his mouth. Steve mumbled while Bess spoke up.

"Starlighter," she said firmly. "It's not a flying saucer."

"Any chance the *Starlighter*," Brooks emphasized the name, "has any weaponry that can be used?"

Portia looked at Steve. They never wanted their craft to be a military aircraft. "It has been repaired, but can't fly with that big ray gun over in the Crater," Portia insisted. "But if there was no threat from that, we *could* find a way to use it to," she paused for the right word, "disrupt other craft.

"It would take time, of course."

Brooks scratched his head. "We'll need some time to take out that big gun they got, anyway. It's a moot point if we can take that thing out even after we take care of those men at the ranch."

The officers and the Truly family stood silently for only a second. Bess spoke first. "So, let's figure out how we're gonna do that."

Bess drew out a large map of the Fields Ranch. It was surrounded by miles of barbed wire, but the main house, the bunkhouse, and the large field where two saucers sat only had a gated fence in the front, according to a soldier with binoculars from high up in the flight tower. The road that ran to the ranch was two miles long, straight and flat and as open as the prairie could be. "They will see us coming as soon as we clear the town."

Bess looked at the thirty men riding the horses on the apron of the airstrip. They were picked because they all had experience on horseback, and were getting comfortable with their new steeds.

"We can use that to our advantage," Bess suggested.

Brooks looked at her, then to the horses, then at the small fleet of cars and trucks.

"Where's Corporal Robinson? Robinson!" Brooks yelled.

"Sir!" came the call of a thin man leaning over a large collection of bags and boxes.

"We got explosives, Robinson?"

"Got all the Comp C, some of the primers were damaged. We're in business, sir," came the answer.

"Good." Brooks turned to Steve. "Just how attached are you to that new Jeep you got there?"

Much later into the night, Bess watched from the protection of darkness as the lights from the town slowly came on. It was late enough that most of the citizens of Three Winds would sleep through what was going to happen soon just outside of town. She stood up in her saddle, with her horse Electra standing still and quiet. Other horses snorted and pawed the ground. They were nervous at being out at night, with strange men on their backs.

Bess had led a group of thirty men and horses on a roundabout route to get to where they were. They waited one hundred yards away from a thin strip of barbed wire strung along the wooden posts that was the east boundary of the Fields Ranch. Already two soldiers had gone out into the darkness to remove the wire. They disappeared into the night within ten feet of Bess's vision. She was only able to see their results when she barely made out tiny pinpricks of light that marked where the posts that had held the wire stood. Red flashlights were buried into the sand next to the posts that marked the open path for the horses.

Bess could see the ranch clearly even though it was far away. Surrounding the house was a mostly decorative split rail fence. The entranceway was guarded by a long tall fence and a closed metal gate that opened electronically from the ranch house. Behind the house, on a grassy lawn, stood two of the saucers that had been in the hidden cavern just hours before. Along the front of the fence were holes blown into the prairie ground. Bess assumed they used those strange atomic weapons. The dirt was piled into mounds, and several moon men stood behind the hills. They all noticeably carried their pistols, pointed toward the entrance and the road beyond.

Bess could see the entire defense easily. The ranch was lit up with a strange green-gray glow from lights strung across the wide open yard of the Fields ranch. Some lights shone out into the empty prairie.

The next lights she saw were car headlights. A long row of vehicles lit up in a chain of lights that rolled quickly from the town toward the entrance road to the Fields Ranch. The vehicles spread out into two rows over the narrow road. They began to drive toward the gate. The long road made the cars look like they moved at a crawl, even though they were flying down the street as fast as the cars would take them.

Bess shifted in her saddle. She was used to fixing problems by action, so sitting still in the darkness while others charged headlong into danger wasn't normal for her. Electra felt Bess's discomfort and pawed the ground, but made no noise. The other horses were on alert, too. Bess could see the ears twitch in the darkness. A few snuffled quietly.

Bess couldn't see the men on horseback except for the occasional outline. They wore strange camouflage ponchos that made them disappear against the sandy prairie. Their faces were done in makeup that darkened their lighter skin and highlighted the dark areas. They looked like photographic negatives of people.

She wondered what these men were thinking. Were they nervous? How many had done something like this before? It seemed odd that there was a group of soldiers ready and only an hour away. She thought about Agent Marsh, the Chair, a simple looking black suit wearing soft spoken man who knew the captain of this group and knew him well. He was a G-Man, a Government Man, but not with the FBI.

Bess shook the thoughts from her head. Time was getting close.

She watched as the cars got closer to the entrance. There still was nothing to see in the darkness but the moving headlights.

Finally, the headlights began to wink out. The cars disappeared into the night, one by one, until all the lights were gone except one lone pair of headlamps that beamed straight out onto the road and the fast approaching gate. The car reached the border where the lights shone out over the open property and the closed metal gate. The moon men gathered at the entrance. They stood behind the barricade with their atomic ray guns drawn and pointed at the car.

Once the car became visible in the lights of the ranch, Bess was able to see the distinct white and red color of the vehicle. It was her family's new Jeep. The paint still shone under the strange glare of the moon men's spotlights. None of the moon men fired their weapons yet. They waited for the Jeep to stop and let out whatever soldiers were planning their foolhardy frontal assault.

The Jeep never slowed.

The Jeep crashed into one side of the gate, embedding itself into the thick stone pylon that made up one side of the entrance gate. For a very brief moment, a mere heartbeat, everyone saw it sit there. Then it exploded in a massive fireball that blew the gate, the pylons, and the entire fence to bits.

"That's our sign," said a sergeant quietly to Bess. Her heart skipped with the words. He had been so still she had forgotten he was there. The horses started out at a quick trot toward the open hole in the barbed wire fence. Bess led the way. Electra was used to the terrain and the night. Bess knew firsthand what the Fields ranch property looked like, where the trucks parked, where it was gravel, sand, or paved, and where a horse might get caught up in a low hung rope or a picket fence.

The distraction at the gate had pulled a lot of the moon men from their hiding places, but they didn't know how to react. They still had no one to fight. As soon as they stopped moving and began to stare out into the darkness, they saw the first of the soldiers moving toward them. The soldiers marched in wavy lines of ten men each. They moved quickly and erratically. From far away, to Bess they looked more like ashen wraiths, dark ghosts borne up out of the plains. As frightening as the soldiers looked that rode with Bess, these were more terrifying. They moved like nothing Bess had ever seen. One would stumble and right himself in a moment, and never slow down the march. They moved with terrifying efficiency toward the well armed moon men.

Now the ranch came to life. The moon men had targets, and the first shots from their ray guns came forth. The weapons spouted out a white beam that created an instantaneous explosion far down into the approaching soldiers. Great clods of dirt flew up, and the soldiers were knocked backwards.

Then they got back up. They began moving again.

More blasts from the moon men had the same effect. The soldiers fell or flew back, then rose back up. Bess and the soldiers had ridden close enough to see the ranch well. The moon men stopped firing. She could see them loading their weapons. The ray guns could only fire one shot before reloading, but there were at least fifty of them firing along the fence.

Finally, just before the line of horses came into the soft gauzy light from the ranch, a huge blast came from a freshly dug hill on the property. The moon men had fired one of their large ray guns out into the ghost soldiers. It burned a line into the prairie, exploding dirt and rock for forty feet across. The soldiers it hit fell down and stayed down this time.

"That's our signal, ma'am," said the sergeant. Bess was surprised how calm he was after seeing the gigantic blast across the line of soldiers. "We needed to know where that big weapon was."

And with that, the entire herd of horses and men, with Bess Truly in the lead, took off at a gallop into the battle of Fields Ranch.

CHAPTER 17

Cavalry Charge!

Bess drew her Zap-Gun as she and the soldiers galloped toward the ranch. The split rail fence turned to splinters as she fired on it to open a path for the soldiers on horseback.

They had been ordered to be noticed. Bess certainly did that. Thirty soldiers on horseback stormed out of the darkness, led by Bess and Electra. Her Zap-Gun burned lightning into the brightly lit ranch. Twenty moon men froze in their tracks, terrified of the galloping nightmare that crashed out of the darkness behind them. They stood still, unsure of what to do. They had fired their weapons and were standing out in the open while the horses thundered toward them. One moon man panicked and ran. Within seconds, the rest took off after him.

The cavalry piled into the long front courtyard. Soldiers began throwing smoke grenades into the holes dug by the moon men. The clouds choked out the light. The strange moon men in their dark cloaks scrambled out while trying to wave the clouds out of their eyes. Bess looked to her right to see the two flying saucers that sat in a grassy field in the back corner of the ranch. They would have to get to those before the saucers took off, but the moon men had to be stopped at the front of the ranch first.

The moon men still tried to battle the soldiers that continued their ghostly march toward the ranch through the open prairie in front of the ranch. One group of soldiers had already reached the small fence that lined the property. They were caught in the wood posts only a hundred feet away as a shot from a ray gun struck the group in the middle. Bess watched as several of the soldiers folded and fell over the rails.

Just then, a strange gauzy cloud floated slowly down in front of her. It was black, but almost transparent. It was there, and not there, at the same time. The cloud fell onto the ground in front of four soldiers on horseback, who stomped into it. The horses drew up short, whinnied and kicked as their hooves were tangled in the strange solid smoke. The soldiers pulled the reins, with one horse rising up to throw its rider. The other three soldiers dismounted and untangled the horses first before helping the fallen rider.

Another four soldiers dismounted and joined them. They pulled from their saddles sets of strange weapons that Bess didn't recognize. One had a large device with big weights on the end. When a moon man popped out of a hole in surprise at the soldiers, he pointed his weapon and fired. It discharged not with a bang, but a muffled *whoosh*, as a net expanded out and slammed into the moon man, throwing him back and pinning him to the ground in his hole.

One of the soldiers yelled, "Keep back from them! Make sure there aren't more!" as the rest spread out to search the nearby holes and bunkers.

A large piece of the gauzy smoke tangled into Electra's reins. Bess grabbed at it and pulled. It turned out to be a spiderweb of fine silk. The smoky cloth split in her fingers.

She saw another cloud of the strange cloth fly into view over the fence and into the lights of the ranch. It lifted up in a strong gust of wind. At the same moment, a line of the ghostly soldiers jumped. They flew into the air, clearing the fence and began a spectral walk through the dark sky, ghosts walking in the night air.

"They're fake!" yelled a corporal on horseback beside her. "They're just paper!"

Bess looked at the paper soldiers, as her head bounced along while Electra ran at a gallop. Now she could see the figures were just shadows and shapes, without detail. The shadows were made up of thin tissue, and pulled by the gossamer webs that flew like kites.

"If those are fake soldiers," Bess wondered, "Where are the real ones?"

A loud explosion answered her question. A flash of bright light and a cloud of dust sent both the far fence corner and a large portion of the prairie flying into the night. White pinpoints of light flashed from the darkness into the opening in the fence. Soft crackles of rifle fire mixed with the shouts of the moon men as they ran in various directions.

Bess saw a clump of fence rail fly through the air and knock down a bright lamp post, sending the area nearby into relative darkness. She and the rest of the horseback soldiers rode closer to the far corner, passing the straggling moon men that were soon caught up in nets or lines shot from Bess's attacking cavalry. Looking out into the darkened area, she saw four of the moon men squinting and staggering around in the dark. They focused on the nearest bright light and began to run toward it. The light was far away, but getting closer with every galloping step of Electra. Bess fired at the lamp. It was a long distance for her to be accurate with her shot, but the static charge reached out to the electricity and wiring like they knew each other. The blue pulse of lightning found the white light. The bulb popped, sending more of the ranch into darkness.

When the light went out, the moon men stopped. They just stood there or staggered around. One tripped and fell, while the others searched for a new bright light.

It wasn't that dark out, Bess thought. There was still plenty of light around, spilling from the house and the large bunkhouse at the far end of the ranch. But the moon men were having a hard time seeing in the dim light. She remembered how bright the cavern was where their secret base was located. The moon men needed bright light.

More soldiers were jumping off their horses now, using nets and smoke to stop and capture the few moon men they passed. "They can't see without the lights!" Bess yelled to the corporal who was keeping up beside her. "We need to take out the lights!" The corporal wheeled his horse around in a wide arc back to the soldiers that dismounted and gave them an order. Bess watched behind her as a soldier drew his sidearm and began firing at the lamps around the ranch, sending the front of the yard deeper into darkness. The soldiers didn't care about how dark it was. They worked well in smoke and dark, appearing like ghostly spirits to fire more of the weighted nets at whatever moon man that appeared before them.

The long front of the ranch was getting shorter by the second. Bess still had more than half of her soldiers with her, and they still had their job to do. From the west out of the darkness and chaos, the bulk of the military force finally appeared, storming over the fence and heading toward the moon men, who were divided, unable to rearm, and in disarray. There was a stampede of horses coming at them from one side, led by a mad and near magical rider shooting blue flame out of the dust, smoke, and darkness. A large body of camouflaged soldiers came from the other side of the ranch. All the while the lights were being turned off one by one, and ghosts were appearing across the entire front of the ranch. The moon men did the only thing left for them to do.

They ran.

Bess and her cavalry stormed around the corner of the ranch just as the remains of the moon men cut and ran toward the closest lit building they could see, the large bunkhouse. Several of the moon men were cut off by the rolling stampede and were trapped in the corner of the ranch, huddling in the dark. They struggled to find their weapons and reload when the last of the horseback soldiers rode by. One soldier wore a small tank on his back, attached to a tube and long nozzle. It looked like a flamethrower, but when he passed, he pulled the trigger to discharge a high pressure spray over the moon men. The liquid turned to a shiny goo that stuck to the men, all over their robes, arms, and hands. They began to shine in the moonlight like they were shellacked. They dropped their weapons from their fingers. When they tried to pick them up, the ray guns slipped like they were made of glass and coated with oil.

The largest group of moon men ran to hide inside the bunkhouse while the soldiers came in to surround the stragglers, trapping them in nets or knocking them down with short barreled weapons that shot out small bean bags that tumbled through the air until they collided with the moon men.

Bess looked behind her as they rode by. She had less than twenty riders left with her, but that was enough. The foot soldiers ran past them as soon as they passed, surrounding the bunkhouse. They began shooting out the lights, and several men began to climb the power pole that led to the bunkhouse. As Bess passed out of view, the lights went out on the bunkhouse.

"Well, that's not my job," Bess thought. She didn't know how the military would handle the remaining moon men barricaded in the house. She had done part of what she was expected. She had distracted the moon men and had led her small force in like lightning to strike at the enemy. Now they just had to move around to take out the flying saucers.

Electra was breathing hard now. They had been at a full gallop since coming in from the dark of the prairie. Even with the explosions and strange sights, Electra and the other horses had performed excellently. But they all would get tired soon. Bess and Electra were used to staying at a full gallop for a long period of time, and they knew each other. The rest of the riders and horses would have a tougher time, but they all would do what they had to do.

The horses and soldiers rode on through the back of the ranch. It was darker there, and it grew blacker by the moment as more power was turned off by the soldiers. But Bess's targets were still well lit. They began to glow even brighter as Bess got closer.

The two flying saucers were getting ready to take off. Twin ray guns extended beneath the cockpits, ready to fire off their lethal beams.

CHAPTER 18

The Desert Hunt

The ray gun of the closer ship ticked its way across the underside of the flying saucer. The opening in the hull glowed green and a loud whine filled the air.

Bess wheeled Electra to the right as she yelled, "They're going to fire! Get out of the way!"

The remaining riders split off left and right just in time as a green blast poured out of the ray gun. The beam tore into the hard packed ground, spouting gravel and dirt into the air. It shot rocks across the horses and riders as they tried to avoid the blast. The riders immediately rode to cover and jumped off the horses. It made the soldiers more difficult targets. It also allowed them to bring their more dangerous weapons to bare on the armored flying saucers. Bullets from rifles and sub-machine guns poured into the metal saucer, sending sparks flying from the ricochets but doing little damage.

Bess and a few soldiers rode close to the Fields' ranch house. A saucer was trying to target the other group of soldiers while the horses rode around it. Both flying saucers were trying to take off, but only the far saucer was able to lift up. The closer one was having difficulty getting power to both the engines and the ray gun. The farther one had no such difficulty. Its pilot applied full power and jumped into the night sky. It wobbled like it was on a string. The powerful lift-off had caused the pilot to lose control and the ship swung around in the night sky. It quickly lost altitude, then bounced on invisible springs. The pilot regained control before starting to head off into the dark prairie.

Bess kicked Electra to a gallop as she aimed her Zap-Gun. She couldn't let the ship get airborne to use its ray gun on the troops on the ground. Or worse, use it on the town. She and three soldiers chased after the rapidly accelerating moon saucer.

The small saucer sped off into the night. Bess and Electra quickly left the other horses behind. She could see the little ship clearly. Its green glow illuminated the saucer.

But the green glow started getting smaller and smaller as the distance grew between them. Bess worried that it would get away, go hide in the night near the moon men's base at the Crater, and then come with the other ships and attack them all from far overhead.

The saucer flew low and fast, kicking up a dark tail as it left a cloud of dust in its wake. The light from the saucer diminished more.

Then it turned.

Bess watched as the saucer made a hard arcing turn across the empty plain. Its gravity powered engines carved a long C shape into the prairie as the exhaust poured out of the saucer. Then it headed back toward Bess.

Horse and rider stopped in the dark plains, far from the battle of Fields Ranch, far from any sort of cover.

She was out in the open, and the moon saucer was now heading directly for her.

Bess wheeled Electra and took off the way she had come. She looked over her shoulder to see the saucer now rapidly closing on her. The green glow of the ray gun began to pulse with a growing intensity. Then it became a glare. Then a loud crash blasted out along with a bright green ray. The ray tore into the soil, reaching out toward Bess as she rode as fast as she could to escape the lethal beam. It chased her, getting closer and closer to Electra's hooves. Just as Bess felt her hair stand on end from the electrical atomic charge, she pulled Electra's reins and took her out of the beam's path.

The beam ripped through the ground where Electra had been moments before. Bess circled Electra around in the darkness as the saucer passed beside them. Scared and shook from the attack, Bess also felt her dander rise. No one attacked her, her horse, or her town. She urged Electra on toward the saucer. It was headed toward the ranch and the soldiers doing battle with the remaining moon men. Bess wasn't going to let anyone else get hurt if she could help it.

At a gallop, she drew her Zap-Gun's sight onto the saucer. She thumbed the power dial up to maximum and fired. The blue light flew out of her barrel into the darkness before popping across the saucer. Bess saw sparks and chips of metal flash off the hull. Even if her shot from far away had done little damage, it got the attention of the pilot. He may have thought he had done away with Bess as he swept his ray gun across the prairie. The saucer slowed, wobbled, and attempted to turn on its axis. The ray gun swiveled underneath, searching for a target in the darkness. Bess rode in a wide arc, using the night as a cover. She kept her finger off the trigger of her Zap-Gun.

Again the saucer's ray gun blasted, reaching out into the empty plains. Dirt tore up from the energy that burned into the ground. The pilot was hunting the darkness for a target, not caring about what he hit.

Bess thought again about how her prairie was full of life. Lizards and bugs lived in the soil where jackrabbits ran and were hunted by hawks and foxes. Every time those moon men tore into the ground, they removed a bit of her home. Everything that they did was wrong, harmful, a work of hate and uncaring. Bess was going to send this one the bill for damage done.

The saucer was now slowly running back east, away from the ranch. Bess continued to circle around, and tightened the circle so that she could come up behind its ray gun. Bess closed in and aimed her Zap-Gun from only fifty feet away. Taking careful aim as she rode, Bess squeezed the trigger.

The blue flame of the Zap-Gun at high power crackled into the base of the ray gun. Metal flew, and braided coils popped and smoked, spewing coolant and whatever noxious magic the moon men pumped out of the ray gun. The ray gun tried to spin, but began to seize.

The saucer began to spin lazily as it worked its way through the gravity it was so unused to. Bess continued to stay behind the pilot. She saw him, now close in the dome of the cockpit. He stared her down, trying to work the sluggish controls and get the ray gun to turn toward Bess. His face was a visage of hate.

Bess squeezed the trigger again. The blue charge crackled across the top of the saucer as it dipped in its sluggish turn. Paint and metal sheared off. A vent ripped apart and clanged across the thick glass dome. Bess was doing damage to the ship, but it was taking too long. She wished she had her friends with her. Together they would have taken the saucer down. Bess, alone, was having a much harder time.

The saucer finally turned toward Bess and Electra. The ray gun could no longer move to aim, and Bess didn't know if it could still fire on her.

She got her answer quickly.

The ray gun blasted above her head as she rode Electra away from the ship at a gallop. The gun couldn't point down without slowing the ship. Bess felt her hair stand on end as the energy bolt passed overhead into the dark.

Bess turned in the saddle, pointed her Zap-Gun, and fired again. Her aim was true, striking the blunt edge of the saucer and cutting a gash into it. With one hand on the reins, trusting Electra, she fired over and over. The saucer couldn't bring the ray gun to bear, and the weapon was having trouble cycling through its reloading process.

Bess rode as fast as she dared in the dark. She hoped to get back to the ranch and any measure of protection. Even the other soldiers would provide some form of support.

Bess looked ahead for a brief moment. As she did, she thought she saw more of those ghost soldiers, the shadowy wraiths that marched into the mill that was the moon men's personal ray guns. Bess guessed some had drifted out into the prairie.

Then they moved.

Three dark figures stood up as she passed to their left. The saucer was closing, and she knew the ray gun would fire again soon. Bess hoped to guess when and dodge the blast. But when the figures moved, she saw them as fully formed. They were the soldiers that had followed her into the plains after the saucer.

Just as the saucer reached them, there was a cacophony of sound as weapons ripped up the night. Bess saw flashes from the muzzles. There was the crisp *crack crack* of an automatic pistol, the deep cough of a shotgun, and finally the *rattlerattle* of a Thompson submachine gun. Bullets flew off the underside of the saucer or rattled around in the vents and intakes. The attack from the darkness sent the saucer spinning off. The pilot didn't know who was shooting now, and could find no good target. He tried to slew the saucer, throwing it into a tall turn into the night sky. Bess and the soldiers watched as it left a trail of smoke and sparks. The green light of its engine was now a more sickening pallor.

It dropped back toward the ground, bouncing hard on the strange invisible supports that flew the saucer. It half flew, half crashed toward the soldiers. They ran in three different directions as the saucer came hurtling down at them. The ray gun popped, and a hole dug into the ground where the soldiers were only heartbeats earlier.

The blast only hit earth. Now the pilot was running slow, his ship hurt, and his weapon failing. And Bess was behind him, riding fast. Electra frothed as she continued her run. The horse sensed the importance of her task, and even though she was tired, she still gave her all. They were able to catch up with the saucer before it could turn again.

Bess took her time aiming. She waited, feeling her heart beating, and settled her breathing. She let herself be calm for a moment. She pointed at the ship as it slowed. She aimed at one of the main thrusters under the saucer and fired. The blue lightning hit directly on the target. Bess held her finger down, sending more power into the saucer, until she was rewarded with a tremendous explosion. The engine shredded and strewed metal across the prairie. Little bits of saucer debris popped into the crusty sand. The saucer wobbled, then flipped onto its front end. It stood up on an edge. The saucer was balanced perpendicular to the ground as it struggled to stay aloft. Then the entire ring threw a halo of sparks. The green lights went out. The ship was crippled.

If fell forty feet straight into the plains, embedding itself into the soil.

Bess finally was able to slow to a stop. She felt Electra panting and heaving under her. Bess watched the soldiers run toward the stricken craft to capture the pilot.

Bess wheeled Electra around. Her horse snorted, huffed, and pawed the ground. Then they started off toward the ranch.

The other saucer was still trying to lift off.

CHAPTER 19

The Hard Way

Electra was able to ride at a trot, but it took an excruciatingly long time to cross the empty prairie. As she closed in on the ranch, Bess could see the remaining saucer still flying at a low altitude. It had only one of its three landing gear up and was smoking copiously out of one of its vents. The ship was not able to lift high off the ground, and it couldn't bring its weapon to bear without using up what little power it had left.

As Bess rode back into the ranch, the saucer crashed into the side of the Fields' house, knocking the tall brick chimney into the home. Bricks spilled from the side of the home like a waterfall of stone.

The soldiers were letting the saucer really have it, but they had to keep moving to stay out of the target of the big ray gun. It had done considerable damage to the rear of the ranch. A storage barn was nothing more than a smoldering bundle of timber, and large trenches had been dug into the hard packed ground. Bullets pinged off the machine's metal hide. The soldiers poured their weapons' ammunition into the flying saucer. But they could only do so much damage. It was starting to gain height. If it could get high enough, one blast from its ray could devastate the troops out in the open around the ranch.

Bess, tired and sore, on Electra, tired and sore as well, waded in to the fight from the darkness of the prairie.

She led Electra through a broken part of the split rail fence to the rear of the ranch. The saucer was slowly working its way out of the remains of the chimney and rising above the roof line of the house. The pilot was trying to move toward the front yard. Bess stopped and aimed at the underside of the saucer. She squeezed the trigger, pouring out a full power blast from her Zap-Gun into a single point on the ship. Metal cracked, melted, and peeled away.

As she fired, three soldiers ran out of the shadows, armed with grenades. The saucer started turning. The pilot had two threats to his ship. He may have not wanted to give up power to use the ray gun that hung underneath his saucer, but the danger was immediate, both for the pilot and for the soldiers trying to bring it down. The soldiers threw their grenades in one of the troughs cut by the ray gun before running for cover.

Bess, farther away, turned Electra and rode back into the open prairie. She didn't know what damage the grenades would do. As she sent Electra in the direction of safety, she waited on the explosions.

It took three seconds for the grenades to burn their fuses and explode. Bess looked over her shoulder to see what happened.

All three went off with a muffled pop. The explosions didn't do much damage, it seemed. Bess heard small metallic pings as metal rang against metal. But the grenades in the trough threw up a large amount of rock and dirt. The saucer's working ducts sucked up the rocks, making the engines whine and ping at high velocity. The rocks were doing massive damage to the insides of the saucer's engines.

The saucer collapsed out of the air, one of its still extended landing legs crushing under the weight of the impact. The pilot tried to apply more power, but the engines wheezed. They were unable to lift the heavy ship with any control. It rose at an unstable angle and then fell. The saucer crashed onto the dirt, then slid across the hard packed gravel road that wrapped around the ranch. There was one high pitched whine, then the saucer gave out a last whimper and became quiet.

With the saucer down, there was a strange and noticeable silence over the ranch. Bess was exhausted from her hard ride and being awake all night. She slumped in the saddle, just for a moment. There were no more moon men running around, shooting their ray guns, no flying saucers about to attack the town. Bess wished her friends were with her, just for support. She got down off of Electra, stretching her sore legs. She rubbed the neck of her horse. "You did a good job, girl," she said soothingly. "We'll get you an extra treat when we get in tonight."

Bess walked Electra around the front of the ranch. No one was stopping her. Some of the moon men were being guarded by soldiers who had changed into thick hooded suits that covered every inch of their bodies. They weren't taking chances with the radioactivity of the moon men.

The corporal that had ridden with Bess on the first attack trotted up on horseback to her as she walked across the front courtyard. "Ma'am," he greeted Bess. He was tired and dusty, but seemed fairly happy with what was a successful mission. "First, your horses are all fine. Most of the men dismounted, and the horses are now in a pen over there," he gestured to a far off darkened corner of the ranch. "We'll arrange for your family to pick them up as soon as possible.

"Also, most of the enemy has been secured. The stockade on the far side of the property where they ran during the attack has been sealed. They don't seem to have any weapons left, and the fight was knocked out of them real quick. We are arranging their surrender, but I would advise you to steer clear of the area until we have them all out and in custody."

Bess was glad to hear this. The soldiers that guarded the few moon men that didn't make it into the bunkhouse stood around anxiously, weapons held ready. There were several hurt by the blasts of the ray guns that were being tended by medics.

"Finally," the corporal went on, "Captain Brooks and Mr. Marsh are in the house. They have captured the officers in charge as well as the owner of the ranch who collaborated with the invaders. They would like to see you." He pointed at the door to the Fields house.

Bess tied Electra to a hitching post and walked up to the house. The corporal ordered a soldier to guard the horse until Bess came back out. "That girl is a hero, private. You treat her as such." Bess assumed he was talking about Electra. "Well," she thought, "he definitely would be right about that." Even though there was a trough nearby, the soldier had opened his canteen and was pouring water out slowly, sharing it with Electra, who lapped happily at the stream of fresh water. He looked up and smiled. Bess noticed how young he seemed. "We look after our own, ma'am," he said with a grin.

"If he's not a cowboy," Bess thought, "he's gonna be."

Bess went straight inside the house.

Inside the living room were people crowded into corners. Two soldiers stood over Mr. Fields, who was looking silently with hate at anyone who made eye contact with him. The fire in his eyes heated up a notch when Bess entered. She knew he hated her father for her family's success in ranching, even though Fields had a much bigger ranch. Mr. Fields had always looked to take over their land, as well as control the town. That might have been his plan for collaborating with the moon men all along.

Nanette and her mother stood in a corner, glaring at Mr. Fields. They seemed displeased at him as much as the others in the room. Nanette caught Bess's gaze and quickly looked down in shame.

Equally far away from both sides of the Fields family sat two moon men, covered in heavy black blankets and what looked like waterproof oilskin cloaks. Two menacing soldiers stood over them, weapons leveled. The soldiers looked like otherworldly cowboys They wore long black dusters that reflected like the oilskin blankets. Over their faces they wore gas masks with hoods.

In the middle of the room sat a makeshift table with a strange set of devices on it. Two soldiers sat at it, listening through headphones, while Captain Brooks and Agent Marsh stood nearby.

"Bess!" Agent Marsh actually smiled and showed emotion. "I'm glad you are alright!"

Captain Brooks turned to her and gave a small tight lipped smile. "Corporal Robinson gave a high accounting of your leadership, ma'am," he said. "He told me you singlehandedly chased down and destroyed a saucer. You have impressed a great number of my men.

"And me, as well," he added, speaking clearly and loudly. Brooks was going to admit he was wrong to doubt her, happily, after what she did tonight.

Agent Marsh quickly turned back into his unemotional self. "We have all the invaders here captured, and they are confessing to their deeds," he glanced over at the two moon men under guard, then continued, "but we need to know where this large weapon is that you described. We need to destroy it so we can land more airplanes to cart away these radioactive goons here." Marsh jerked an uncaring thumb at the moon men. "Will you be able to guide us to the location? You're not injured, are you?" Marsh thought about what he was asking. Bess was a civilian, and a teenager at that, even if she had helped lead an attack that captured an invading army without any soldiers being killed. He needed to be respectful of her.

But Bess was tough as any New Mexico cowgirl would be. "I'm good. I'm a little sore, but Electra is up for another ride. Yeah, I can show you, no problem."

"No. Listen, it is a problem," Agent Marsh said. "This is all dangerous. You need to know what you are getting into. This is a much bigger threat. And those guys," again he pointed at the moon men, "don't care what happens to you."

Bess looked at the moon men, angry and miserable at being caught. "They didn't care what happened to my town, my friends, anyone. They were only out for themselves. We have to look out for each other. We have to protect my home. *I* have to protect my friends.

"I'll do whatever it takes."

One of the men at the table stood up and showed Agent Marsh a piece of paper. "We're getting lots of chatter from them on their intercom channel. They are trying to find out what is happening here. Lots of questions, lots of unsure stuff. It's really fast and we can't understand all of it.

149

"But then there's this." he flipped a piece of paper. "It's on a different channel. It's not quite as clear, like it's longer distance. Not much talk, but we got questions about time, when is something happening, asking for help or supplies, the words are still unclear." Bess tried to see what was on the pad. It looked like a jumble of letters, and English underneath.

"Then we got this," he showed the pad to Marsh.

Marsh looked at the pad, then read it out loud. "*Vahshnavf Rasche esh comnir.*"

He looked over at the two moon men. They looked decidedly more content at those words.

"Something's coming," Agent Marsh said. He looked bitterly at the two captives. They wouldn't give him anything, he knew. But then, they already told him something. Whatever it was, it was bad.

"We've got to get you moving," he said to Bess.

Ten minutes later Bess was riding Electra alongside an open topped Jeep and a truck taken from the Fields garage. The trucks rode in darkness, with no headlights on, which felt eerie to Bess. What was worse was the strange contraption the driver wore over his eyes. He had on large goggles that looked out into the dusty road that led to the Crater. Above her another soldier held a large domed light that emitted no beam that Bess could see. Somehow the driver could see where he was going in the dark.

Corporal Robinson rode next to her. He explained to her that the driver was seeing infrared light from the giant bulb, and could see in the dark. He didn't bother to explain the science. There wasn't a need, and they didn't have time.

The driver of the truck behind them had a similar set of goggles on. In the back rode a small number of soldiers, including two specialists in demolition. Nestled in the back of the truck was enough explosives to blow the giant ray gun to smithereens.

Or it could blow both vehicles to bits, Bess thought.

Slowly they drove over the rutted dirt road that led toward the Crater. They were far away from the town and the stars shown brightly in the black sky. Bess wondered if they could be spotted by starlight.

As the trucks rounded the wide long turn that arced around the low hills and mountains that formed the Crater, she realized she didn't need to be worried about that.
She needed to be worried about something much, much worse.

The giant ray gun sat out in the middle of the Crater, towering up in the empty bowl that was the basin around the jagged hilltops. It sat on its large set of tractor treads, so that the weapon could be rolled out from the hidden cavern carved out of the mountains nearby. On the front, lit by bright white bulbs on tall lamps, stood a team of the moon men inside the wide glass bubble that was the control platform for the ray gun. They monitored a large screen and a bank of switches. From the ray gun to the mountain ran a

151

line of giant cables. They lay on a hard road bed that entered into the dark shadowy curtain on the sheer cliff of the mountain. "That must be the other side of the hidden base we found," thought Bess. She remembered the strange wavering wall of false stone, a projection of rock that hid the giant opening where the ray gun and flying saucers were stored. What was still inside, past that darkened wall, was a mystery. There could be hundreds of armed moon men, or more flying saucers. Bess knew that they had at least two of the flying craft hidden somewhere.

The trucks stopped far off so they wouldn't be spotted or heard as they got closer. The rest would be done on foot. "The hard way," the corporal had muttered.

The soldiers gathered into small groups to discuss their tactics and plan to destroy the giant ray gun. "They can't see well in the dark, it looks like," said Corporal Robinson as he glanced at the bright lights that lined the concrete road and the control deck of the ray gun. "We could approach pretty close without being seen. What can you do?" He addressed his question to another officer. Bess noticed that even though some soldiers outranked others, they looked to the person with the experience and skill to do their part. Clearly, the corporal was in charge of the approach, while the officer, a lieutenant, was the explosives expert.

"We could cut their power. It looks like they run that thing from inside the mountain. Those cables may be a weak point."

"Or a hard spot. What about damaging the controls?"

"We don't know if that thing has its own power source."

"We can create a distraction there," the corporal pointed to a dark point to the east. He pulled out binoculars to examine the ray gun. "Then come from the opposite side, damage the supports, contain the control group with smoke and the MDS," he pointed at another of those weird spray guns they had used at the ranch, "then clear and Comp C the thing to bits." Bess didn't know what Comp C meant, but she guessed it had something to with a very large explosion, based on the corporal's description.

"What about the flying saucers?" Bess asked.

The soldiers turned together toward Bess. They had forgotten she was there.

"What flying saucers?"

Bess pointed toward the hidden cliff. "There has to be at least two more of those flying saucers in there. They had five when I went in there."

In all the excitement, the soldiers had not considered there were more of the saucers to contend with.

"That's a bigger problem. Those things are tough to bring down. If one gets up high enough, we won't be able to stop it." He looked at Bess and her Zap-Gun. "You're the only one to ever shoot down a flying saucer. I don't think we can ask you to take that much of a risk on two more."

Bess considered what she had done. She and Aurora had together destroyed one, she had chased down and taken out one of the two from the ranch, with help, and the third one had been mostly destroyed by...

"I've got an idea. Just how much explosive do you have?"

Even in the dark, Bess could see the demolitions team grin with white teeth like sharks in deep.

CHAPTER 20

Hills Of Destruction

An excruciating hour later, small groups of soldiers were scattered around the Crater. Six men hid far off in the dark prairie, while three were much closer to the ray gun. They slowly crept forward in the darkness to demolish the weapon as soon as they got the chance. Three more soldiers were crouched down behind a group of trees. If their quiet groans and yawns were any prediction for Bess, all the soldiers must have been sore and tired.

She was sure how she felt. Exhausted.

It was the middle of the night, Bess was sore from riding her horse, and now she was covered in dust and sand from being out climbing the hills that bordered the Crater. They were the smallest of the ridge, barely one hundred feet tall, but covered with boulders and loose rock that had slipped under her boots and scratched at her jeans.

Now they all waited. If everything worked, they would be rid of the flying saucers, the ray gun would be destroyed, and the moon men stopped.

"That's a big 'if'," Bess thought. "At least then I can get some sleep."

Bess looked at the other soldiers with her. They were all dirty and tired, too. It didn't take long for them to go from fighting an invasion from outer space to wanting to win just to get to bed.

One of the soldiers handed Bess a half full canteen of water. She whispered, "Thanks," and drank it greedily. Wiping her mouth, she handed it back. The soldier, a young private, waved it off. "Finish it," he whispered back, "Water doesn't do any good in the canteen."

The soldier looked at his watch. "Almost time," he warned. They looked out over the open basin of the Crater. Most of what they would do would require watching and waiting. And hoping everything else went right.

Bess stared up into the dark cliffs of the small hills they had just come from. She was able to make out two small reflectors, and a splash of dimly glowing paint that marked two targets. Her job was not going to be easy, but everything else hinged on it being successful. She kept trying to look away from the bright lights of the Crater. They blinded her from the night, but she couldn't help it. Once the flying saucers came out, she had to be ready.

Electra snorted quietly, tied to a tree behind her.

"Any moment now. Watch for the lights out there. We won't see the sappers until after the guards there move off." The private looked out through small binoculars. He pressed them hard into his eyes, trying to will the scene he was watching to start happening. Another soldier anxiously held a wire in his hands while the the third soldier guarded a small detonator. They would have to work fast when the flying saucers came out.

They waited.

Bess felt the soldiers almost relax when after two minutes nothing happened.

Then, "Here we go," said the private. To punctuate the sentence, a popping sound echoed across the prairie. Bess saw, far off to the east in the dark, a series of white flashes, like from the muzzles of rifles. They were so far away that the sound reached her long after the last flash occurred. Then more flashes. This got some of the moon men running. Several jumped off the ray gun and began to pull out their small atomic pistols. They didn't know who it was that was shooting at them, and they looked confused. There were more flashes, then sparks flew up all around the ray gun. The moon men ducked for cover, jumping off the machine and trying to hide.

"It's magnesium. Makes a lot of sparks and scares them," the private said.

It certainly scared the moon men into ducking to the ground. They all scurried away from the control bubble of the ray gun. One fired his ray pistol into the darkness. The explosion sent up smoke and dirt into the air, but did no damage. There were no soldiers there. It was another distraction, like the ghost soldiers that marched across the plains during the attack on the ranch. The soldiers were far off, waiting in the brush of the prairie.

With all the moon men off the ray gun now, the other troops moved in from the opposite side. They stood up, impossibly near. Bess was surprised how close they had gotten without being noticed. A soldier began to shoot a sticky glue all over the deck where the moon men had just left. In moments the entire deck was covered with an expanding foam. Another soldier threw smoke grenades into the foam, where they stuck and sizzled, throwing out a thick cloud of gray fog.

The moon men turned, tried to climb back on, but found their way blocked by the sticky foam. The smoke made it difficult to breathe and see. One moon man simply crouched down beside the ray gun and tried to hide. Without any direction to look or run, he covered his head and hoped no one would see him.

The third soldier was climbing up the ray gun, where large supports moved the heavy weapon. He worked feverishly to attach explosives to the braces that pointed the ray gun upward.

From the mountainside, down the long path that led from the entrance of the mountain to the ray gun, a large group of moon men started to pour out of the hidden opening. Bess thought the soldier on the ray gun would jump down and run. But he barely looked up before going back to work. At the same moment, there were soft puffs of smoke from out of the darkness, followed by quiet pops as the sound traveled across the open plains. The pathway was filled with explosions and smoke. Corporal Robinson's group had finally engaged. The smoke confused the moon men. Bess watched the soldiers run out into the open of the long row of lights, in between the smoke and the ray gun. From so far away, she could barely see them as they worked on the big set of cables that ran along the pathway. But they worked quickly. One soldier waved his arm for them to move, and they ran back off into the darkness The whole movement took less than thirty seconds.

Ten seconds later there was a tremendous explosion as the path filled with a shower of sparks and flames. The lights on the poles pulsed and dimmed, then went dark. The lights winked off rapidly. The area was plunged into darkness, made worse by the blinding flash.

Bess could only guess what happened next. There was another explosion, with a series of loud booms. The ray gun was being destroyed. Her eyes adjusted slowly. She was aided by the moon men, running out into the smoke and darkness, waving bright spotlights into the night. The beams searched through the smoky air, but did nothing to help them find the soldiers. All the lights did was create an eerie glowing fog that didn't fit in with the New Mexico prairie.

Through the smoke and lights, Bess could see the shadow of the ray gun, towering into the night. The big weapon still stood. A bright flash popped off from the far side of the ray gun, and Bess saw the moon men near it run off into the dark.

There was another muffled boom. The bottom of the ray gun sat on a gigantic circular plate that allowed it to swivel around to target aircraft. Smoke flew out from under the plate. The ray gun dropped straight down onto the big tractor treads. Then the braces began to topple. Slowly at first, the supports gave way. Then it tumbled, falling down onto its side. The big tractor treads were pulled over as the whole thing fell with a crash. Bess felt the impact as a muffled thump in the ground even as far away as she was.

It took a moment for them to realize they had succeeded. The giant ray gun was down. Destroyed. Bess looked at the private next to her, expecting to see a contented smile. He was still staring straight out into the night, at the mountain side.

The cliff was partially hidden by the dust that was stirred up from all the explosions, but it was softly lit by stars and the few lights the moon men shone into the night.

Then the cliff became dark. And the mountain got darker and darker. Then a tall bright sliver of light parted the mountain. The curtain was opening. Light poured out onto the Crater, illuminating the big ray gun, laying crushed and lifeless in the middle of the basin.

A hazy shadow stretched out over the basin from inside the mountain. Then another appeared.

Bess saw two flying saucers floating slowly out into the Crater.

"We're up to bat," said the private.

CHAPTER 21

Dust And Moonlight

Off in the prairie, one of the vehicles that brought the small group of soldiers started up and began to drive away. The headlights glared out into the prairie over the bumpy dirt path. It was easy to spot by the two flying saucers as it drove off into the night.

The two ships rose up, their engines pulsing, sending their dull green glow out into the night sky. They flew haltingly, still unaccustomed to the Earth's gravity. Then they stabilized, and both dropped their ray guns from inside the hulls. The pointed weapons swiveled toward the disappearing truck. The ray guns glowed as they poured power into them. Then both fired.

The two bright green rays cut through the dark and dust. The light made streaks on Bess's eyes. In an instant, the truck went up in a tremendous crash. It kept rolling for a moment as the cab burned.

The two flying saucers now moved slowly forward. They had expended their weapons and would take time to reload, as well as regain their power. The soldiers had seen that the ships were devastating in their destructive ability, but could not move quickly after firing.

"Just what we wanted," said the private. He looked at the other soldiers and said, "Play ball!"

Bess jumped up and ran to Electra. She untied her horse as the other two soldiers began attaching the wires to the detonator.

"Ten seconds!" Bess said loudly, "Don't you wait for me! I'll be ready!" She rode off to the dark side of the hills where they had been less than an hour before.

Bess and Electra covered the open ground quickly, Electra charging at a gallop. The horse was confident and sure footed in the prairie sand, and felt the importance of the task. Bess looked to her left and up on the hill. There, even in the dark, two reflectors glistened. Around them, wrapped over large boulders, were spirals of explosive cord. It was a rope that burned at high speed, so fast the eye couldn't see it. Attached to the cord was as much explosive as they could jam into the hillside rocks and rubble.

Bess was counting to ten in her head but as excited as she was, her count was fast. She got to twelve before the soldiers set off their charges. On top of the hill, another set of bright lights sparked off. They were triggered by the soldiers down at the bottom of the hill. Once they fired, the soldiers at the bottom, still down by the ray gun, would hit the flying saucers with whatever they had, machine guns, pistols, rocks if they had to. Anything so that the flying saucers felt like they were being attacked from the ridge line from where the lights came. They needed to be high enough to see the flashing lights, and drawn from the Crater so that they would fly over the edge of the ridge. Bess could no longer see them, but she could see their green glow.

It was getting brighter.

Bess pulled her Zap-Gun and spun her power selector down to a low setting. She only wanted to make some light, a little spark, to keep the saucers moving and interested. She couldn't hit her targets yet. A thin blue crackle of light flew up into the sky.

All the flashes and explosions, along with the lightning from Bess's Zap-Gun, attracted the flying saucers.

They began to climb up the low ridge, looking for the target that was shooting at them. One cleared the ridge. Its ray gun hung under the saucer, swiveling and looking for something to shoot. They both had to be over the ridge and over the two reflectors before Bess could fire.

They began to crest the ridge and turn toward her. "Too soon," Bess thought, clucking at Electra to get her moving. "If they fire now..." Bess didn't finish the thought.

The first of the two saucers started to come down the hill. The other was still climbing over the low peaks. Bess couldn't wait. She saw the first saucer pass over the low boulders. The reflector sparkled brightly under the green glow. It was bright enough that Bess could see the spiral of the explosive cord on the rock. She stopped Electra, spun her Zap-Gun up to full power, aimed, and fired.

From this distance, it was a difficult shot. Even with Electra still, the balance of Bess in a saddle and on a horse made the aim demanding. She let her breath out slowly, and squeezed the trigger.

The bolt cracked out over the distance. For a split second, Bess thought she missed. The blue beam hit the rock, but didn't ignite. Then, the entire rock crackled into a giant *whoosh*. The explosives lit off and threw up a huge cloud of rocks and dirt. They were immediately sucked into the saucer. It first flew high up in the air, propelled by the explosion. Its underside was ripped and torn from the explosives. Metal hung off the bottom in jagged bits. Then the ship began to fall.

The saucer was thrown back by the explosion. It stood on its edge, where the engines couldn't push away from the earth. Without any support, it slipped down the other side of the hill. It crashed and skidded down the cliff side, disappearing from view.

Bess couldn't wait to watch the damage of the first saucer. The second one knew where she was. It was already lifting higher and moving faster. The ray gun turned in her direction.

Bess squeezed Electra, sending her into a fast trot. She didn't bother to aim. She just pointed at the other reflector and fired, squeezing the trigger. She held it down, pouring out blue lightning until it hit the exploding cord.

The saucer had already passed the explosion when it finally went off. Rocks still pounded the underside of the saucer's hull. Several were sucked into the engines with a loud whirring clang. The saucer wheezed and dipped. It quickly lost power and height, but was already past the hillside as it slid down toward the prairie below.

It was sliding straight toward Bess and Electra. Bess stirred her horse to escape from the wounded craft. The ray gun at the bottom of the ship hummed, glowed, and then fired. At the same time, the front of the ship dipped slightly, and the beam tore into the sand beneath the flying saucer. Bess took off into the darkness to escape the lethal beam.

The saucer dipped low enough to touch the ground, then with a surge of power, it flung itself upward and forward. The craft closed quickly on Bess, propelled forward by the strange unseen forces that lifted the flying saucer. It was able to get close enough that its dull green glow lit up the prairie as well as Bess on horseback.

Bess looked over her shoulder as she rode. The saucer was so close she could see the pilot inside. His face was concentrated with hate. Pale skin surrounded dark black eyes, with a tight thin helmet stretched over his head. He leaned on the controls as if to will the saucer forward and cut into horse and rider.

Bess did the only thing she could. She pulled the reins hard and turned Electra to the right. The horse cut easily across the sandy prairie. Electra dug in her hooves, spun around like she was rounding a barrel, and accelerated away.

The pilot couldn't respond quickly, and the saucer hurtled out into the darkness. It turned in a wide looping arc while its engines coughed and strained. "This one isn't going down easily," Bess thought as she rode off, hopefully toward the support of the soldiers, or at least to find protection amidst the few trees and rocks near the hills. It would mean slowing down, which meant the saucer would catch up.

Behind her, the saucer turned. It was heading back the way it came, using the light from the engines to search the prairie. It slowed as it turned bright spotlights on, burning into the night. "They really do have a hard time seeing in the dark," thought Bess. "Those bright lights are definitely going to make it easier to find us."

Bess had to find protection. The hills, trees, and the Crater all stretched out before her now. She could see the burning remains of the first flying saucer casting a shadow over the hill where it had crashed. Farther away, the truck that the saucers had blown up burned to low glowing embers. It had been set off to distract the saucers, and get them to fire their weapons at it. Bess knew it took time to reload or recharge the big ray guns on the saucers, but that time was up.

"And so is mine," she feared. The saucer might have been hampered by the damage from the explosion, but it was still able to close on Bess. It looked like the pilot had her now.

With no reason left to hide, Bess pulled her Zap-Gun and fired at full power. She knew it would take more

than one blast to knock the ship out of the sky, but she wasn't going down without a fight. She squeezed the trigger.

The blue blast ripped through the night sky, tearing into the metal, pulling off paint, then the thick sheet armor. She kept her finger down.

Suddenly, her electric charge sparkled with tiny stars. A trail of yellow sparks circled the blue lightning in a spiral, as a thin line of smoke ripped across her shot. An explosion blasted across the hull of the ship. Bess let loose of the trigger to see what happened. A ball of light and heat burst out on the hull of the ship, tearing its front apart. The pilot's canopy split at the ring around the base and flew off into the darkness. She saw the pilot, ducked down in his seat, look up in wonder for a heartbeat, before grabbing at dead controls.

The saucer moved silently through the air, for only a second. Then it plowed into the soft sand of the prairie. Bess and Electra turned to avoid the craft as it dug a trench through the earth before coming to a stop, smoldering, twisted, and broken.

Bess looked over at the small trees and rocks where she had hid only moments before. The burning wreckage lit up the prairie. Bess could see one of the soldiers lowering an empty rocket launcher.

CHAPTER 22

Annie Oakley Of The Sky

"So, how'd you figure out how to take down those UFOs?" a soldier asked.

The troops stood around a bend in the river, near where Bess and her friends had camped. Bess tried to figure out how long ago that had been. Electra drank from the stream, while a small group of soldiers leaned against the trees near the arroyo, or simply slept on the ground. More soldiers had come in to guard the moon men left in the cavern. Bess ate a soft and doughy cupcake from a can that one of the soldiers had given her from his backpack. She swallowed and said, "Back at the ranch, Agent Marsh said that I was the one who brought down the flying saucers. That's not really true. The one at the Fields Ranch, I mean, I helped, but it was you guys," she waved a sticky finger around in the darkness, taking in the soldiers around her, "that really did it. They threw those grenades, and the rocks and metal all got sucked up into the engines, tearing them up.

"You know what FOD is?" Bess asked. The soldier said nothing. "Foreign Object Damage. My dad's on it all the time. It's stuff that can get sucked up into a plane's engine and tear it up. We just knocked those saucers down with some FOD.

"And some help from you guys," Bess finished her cupcake, crushed the can, and stuffed it back into the soldier's pack.

It was still dark. Bess was surprised at how much had happened all in one night. She looked to the east. Even this early in the morning, the very thin first slivers of light shone over the horizon. All the stars still twinkled on and off in the night. The low rays of the sun wouldn't be up for hours yet.

She saw two sets of stars that moved along the horizon. Squinting and rubbing her eyes, she was able to focus enough to see they were headlights, turning off the main road. One, two, three vehicles sped through the dirt road toward the Crater. One of them peeled off from the others and started heading, off road, straight toward them.

The soldiers woke up. Bess imagined that they were able to sense danger in their sleep. They began to rise and gather their weapons. "Easy," said the soldier who had been talking with Bess. "We're not at war with anyone who drives a car here, remember. If they made it this far without someone stopping them, they are probably friendlies." The soldiers relaxed a little, but none of them put their rifles down.

It wasn't until the car got closer that Bess recognized the familiar blaring sound from the engine. "It's okay! Those are my friends! Jesse!" Bess knew the sound of Jesse's old Ford like she knew the prairie itself.

The orange dune buggy tore into the sand. It looked like a giant insect, with its lights searching out the night for a drink of water from the stream. It didn't slow down until it plowed sideways into the sand, slewing the car in a skid.

"Bess!" screamed a girl's voice.

"Hey, queen of the prairie!" called out a boy's voice.

"Bess, girlie!" one more girl's voice.

"Thank goodness!" came a woman's voice. "Get me out of this bomb." Bess recognized that voice, too. It was her mom. She had ridden in Jesse's Ford to get out to Bess as quickly as possible.

Soldiers pointed flashlights onto the old Ford. Aurora and Lydia were helping Portia out of the front seat, while Jesse grinned. "I told you I could get you to her faster in the Desert Cadillac. I didn't say it would be comfortable."

Portia didn't care. Once out, she ran over to Bess and hugged her. "Are you hurt, hon? You're not injured, are you?"

"I'm fine, Mom," Bess blushed. "I'm glad to see you! Where's Dad?"

Portia motioned over her shoulder. The other lights had slowed. One stopped far away on the dirt road, while the other crawled across the prairie toward them at a snail's pace. "Your father is in the Jeep. He can't travel as fast due to his injured arm." Portia hugged her daughter close. "Careful, Mom, don't break my arm, too!" she laughed, and hugged her back.

The rest of the Zap-Gun Rangers stood back from the family reunion, waiting for them to be done.

"Well, it looks like this party was a real gas," said Jesse, looking around at the soldiers, with a crunched flying saucer torn into the earth in the background. "You guys really went for pinks."

"You can say that again," said Bess.

"Okay, spill," said Aurora.

"Yeah, what's the story?" said Lydia.

So Bess spilled. She told the entire story. The girls were appropriately stunned, and Jesse threw in just the right amount of hip lingo to make Portia squint and frown. It was his true medium and great talent, next to driving across the plains.

By the time Bess finished, one of the Jeeps from the C Bar M pulled up. Steve Truly, his arm in a sling and cast, hopped out and ran to his daughter. With his good arm he grabbed Bess and hugged her.

"Way to go, kiddo! I'm so proud of you! You alright, right?" He let go long enough to look at her in the light of the headlamps and flashlights.

"I'm fine, Dad. A little tired," which was an understatement. She was beat.

"I bet you are, my little Mustang," he looked at Bess and spoke softly now. He knew how draining this could be. It would be even harder on a teenager. But Steve knew his daughter, and knew she would accomplish great things, do the right thing, always ready to find the answer and solve the problem. And he knew as a father he could help solve some of those problems, too.

"Let's get you and your friends home. It's time for bed."

"I'm gonna need," Bess spoke, then was interrupted by a long unstoppable yawn, "aahhhh, a shower, too."

"C'mon, in the Jeep. You ride with us," said her father. "One a you fellas can bring the horse over to the road? I'll send a trailer to pick her up."

With everything secure, and the moon men stopped, Bess snuggled into the back seat of the Jeep. She fell asleep by the time they hit the main road.

Two hours later, she woke up, still tired, with a pasty taste in her mouth. She hadn't even made it to her bed. She had just flopped down on the downstairs sofa and fallen asleep with her boots on. The quiet and narrow murmurs that came from her hallway had been just uncomfortable enough to wake her.

"We are trying to figure out what it is," said a voice.

"Do we need to evacuate?" another voice spoke.

"How much time do we have?"

"Can we fight back?"

Bess stretched and yawned. If nothing else, she was going to get her boots off and go upstairs to her bed. After getting up, she saw through sleepy eyes her parents talking with Agents Phillips and Marsh. "What's going on?" she asked while rubbing her eyes.

"Honey, we think something else is coming," said her father.

"We're trying to figure out what it is, and what we can do about it," continued her mother.

A soldier ran in the door. He pulled up short, looked around for someone to salute, but didn't find anyone. "Sirs, ma'am, um," he looked at Bess, gave up on trying to acknowledge everyone, and said, "The Captain wants to see you all." He then hurried out the door. The four adults barged out of the screen door right behind him. Bess, still groggy, took a heartbeat to catch up.

It took less than two minutes to get back to Hangar One, where the troops had created a makeshift base. In the middle were tables full of electronics. Some belonged to the Army, while others had been taken from the moon men. A large screen lit up near what looked like a radio communications set that was clearly not part of the military's general issue. Bess figured it was something taken from the cavern.

"We haven't heard much, mostly calls for contact. Pretty simple stuff. No answers from this end, of course," said one of the soldiers who was listening in on headphones.

"Any word on what it is that's coming?" asked Captain Brooks. He squinted into the morning light. The soldier didn't respond, just nodded toward the far wall.

On cue, two soldiers in full radioactive protection turned away from a lone prisoner, a sweating and scared moon man. Bess looked at him, thinking, "More like a Moon Boy. He looks so young." The captive looked like a sixteen year old kid, and he looked terrified.

The soldiers took off their garb outside a small boundary wall, then went behind a screen. They had to follow a radiation protocol. The Truly family had a similar but more complex setup near their mine.

Captain Brooks tapped his foot and *hrumphed* while waiting for the men to come out. He finally gave up and shouted, "What did he say?!"

The soldiers spoke through the barriers to the captain. "He's a conscript, sir. He said his family didn't want him to go, but they forced him. They are trapped deep under the moon's surface."

"Did he say what '*Vahshnavf Rasche*' means?" asked Captain Brooks.

"It doesn't have a meaning. That's what threw us," said the other soldier. They finally came out from behind the screen. "He finally explained it to us."

"It's a name, sir."

"It's the name of their ship," explained the first soldier. "It translates to something like a base ship or father ship.

'*Vahshnavf*' means something like that. It's like a big mothership, is best we can figure."

Brooks looked concerned. "What does '*Rasche*' mean?"

The two soldiers looked at each other. They spoke in a somber tone. "Revenge."

If the group of people standing the the hangar needed time to let the name and meaning set in, they didn't get any. Someone manning the electronics yelled out, "Got it!"

A collection of soldiers and civilians and government agents gathered around the big screen in the middle of the hangar. "We couldn't figure much out on this thing until we got that name, sir," explained the operator. "At first we thought it was a radar screen, but it's not."

Steve Truly looked at the big circular screen set up over the table in the middle of all the electronics. They were all items taken from the moon men, and they seemed to communicate with the flying saucers or to and from the base in the Crater. The big screen was less obvious to them. It looked like a radar screen, but picked up small points of light with strange writing on them. "They're transponders," he said.

"Yup, uh, yessir," said the operator. "We are picking up signals from two of the saucers that cowgirl put paid on," he looked up and saw that the "cowgirl" he referred to was standing near him. "Oh, sorry ma'am, no offense," he said with a touch of his hat.

"None taken," Bess said proudly. She figured he hadn't said anything wrong.

"So, two of them are down, but the electronics are still running some. They have a small signal, here," he pointed, "and here, near their base out by the mountains."

Two small blips gave off weak signals and had a short code in the moon language of strange wiggled lines.

"But when we look for what they just said," he keyed in more of the strange language, "this happens."

Near the top of the screen, a dull yellow disc appeared. With every blink, it moved closer toward the center. And, compared to the tiny blinking lights near the center, it was very, very big.

"How far away is that?" asked Steve.

"The way it's moving," answered the radar operator, "less than an hour."

This put most of the group into confusion. No one knew what the craft was. They only knew it was large and getting close. Only Portia Truly seemed to stay calm while everyone figured out what to do. Captain Brooks screamed to get soldiers to interrogate more moon men, and Agent Marsh asked to call nearby Holloman Air Force base for aircraft. When Brooks asked if they had any weapons to shoot it down Portia spoke up.

"I have what you need," she said simply.

Everyone stopped. "You asked for air cover when you lost most of your weapons." She jerked a thumb at the wrecked airplane on her airstrip. "While you were out, we did some work to the Starlighter."

"You got it working, Mom?!" Bess was surprised and ecstatic.

"I've done better than that," she said. "We changed the discharge point on the bottom. We can fire a directed static charge while flying. It will limit our flight time by about ten minutes less, but we should be able to use the Starlighter to knock out power to their ship, or at least limit its power."

"Well," Captain Brooks was doubtful, "it's better than nothing, but we don't have anyone who can pilot..."

"Um, Alan," interrupted Agent Marsh, "I think they already have a pilot."

Brooks looked at Steve Truly. "No offense, but you're not flying with a broken arm."

"I don't think he meant my husband, Captain," said Portia tersely.

Brooks looked at Portia, seeing her glance sideways. He followed her gaze, straight to Bess.

She smiled and said, "Well, I am the only cowgirl here who has taken down those flying saucers." She nodded at the radar operator, who had called her a cowgirl a moment ago.

He grinned at her and said, "Nice shootin', ma'am."

CHAPTER 23

Dancing By Starlight

Bess climbed into the Starlighter. She knew they would be flying by the seat of their pants. There was no information about the approaching moon saucer, except that it was much bigger than the little flying saucers she had dealt with the night before. The sun was beginning to rise over the far horizon. Orange light burned into the purple morning sky, and the lights of stars were beginning to turn off in the east. Bess kept one eye into the lightening morning sky, on the lookout for a star that shouldn't be there.

Behind her, Portia settled into the other seat. With Bess's father injured, someone had to manage the engine and power supply while Bess flew. The civilian radio crackled with a voice from the hangar.

"We'll alert you to angle, direction, and time, as soon as we have a target," sang the voice.

Outside, Bess looked out the window into the hangar. Her father stood there, looking nervous but smiling. He would rather be in the cockpit than Bess, she knew that, but he had faith in her. There was no one else that knew how to fly the Starlighter, and no plane that could maneuver as well nor fly as fast. But until they knew where the big saucer, the *Revenge*, would be, Bess had to sit in the Starlighter, unpowered, silent, but ready to take off. They couldn't afford to use any extra power.

So Bess waited.

She looked at her mother, already strapped into the copilot's seat. Her mother looked back, reading Bess's mind. "You'll be fine, dear. When they find out who is coming for them, those moon people are the ones who will be nervous."

As if on cue, the radio crackled with Steve Truly's voice. "We got'em, kiddo! Coming from the east, bearing one zero one, and hot. Dropping fast."

"Thanks, Dad," Bess called back. "Let's light this thing!"

Portia gave the signal to launch. The outside ring began to spin, quickly reaching a high speed. They weren't messing around with tests now. Bess knew the Starlighter would fly. All the lights came on in the cockpit. "Ready for take-off," Bess called in.

"You're clear, Bess. Go get'em. And remember, they're ridin' Shetlands."

Bess laughed. That was her father's way of telling her to be careful. "Shoot low, they're riding Shetlands!"

"Ready?" she said to her mom. "You're the pilot," came Portia's reply.

Bess pressed the main power button. Immediately she felt the rapid *thumpthumpthump* come from below where the engine delivered the controlled explosions to propel the Starlighter. Bess heard her mother have a sharp intake of breath. Flying in the Starlighter was not like flying in any other kind of airplane.

But Bess couldn't fly softly. She couldn't take it easy. "I'm going to put us up high so we can see it better. We can't wait for it to come to us." Bess leaned on the throttle, twisting it to full, and pushed the controls to fly the Starlighter to the east.

She and Portia scanned the morning sky. Every star might be the light from the big space ship. Every cloud might hide it. Bess, with her sharp eyes, found it seconds before her mother.

"Got it," she said, keeping the lift on to propel the Starlighter closer and closer. Once she got high enough, Bess cut the engine completely. The regular *thump* heartbeat of the Starlighter fell silent. She pulled the handle that opened the control flaps around the cockpit, and the Starlighter began to slowly orbit down from the night sky.

Portia looked at Bess, uncomfortable at the loss of power. "What are you doing?" She clung to the armrest of the seat.

"If we go in fast and hot, they will see us. This way we just coast in over them. Hopefully, they won't see us."

Portia sat quietly. Just because it was a good idea didn't mean she liked it.

With the Starlighter at an angle and slowly gliding down, the two had time to observe the space ship as it came closer. From out of the morning twilight, the *Revenge* stormed out from the dark sky. Even in the black horizon of night, the big space ship poured out smoke from the exhausts, leaving a hazy contrail in the atmosphere. It creased the morning light, and appeared as a big dull disc in the sky. The *Revenge* tore out of the night, into the sunrise heading straight toward Three Winds.

"What do their weapons look like?" asked Portia. She had only seen the small hand held pistol.

"They pop out the bottom of the smaller ships," said Bess. "They're six, maybe eight feet long. Shoots a green energy bolt. It may be different on this thing."

They flew on in silence. There was nothing much to say. Bess kept an eye on her air speed and altimeter. Occasionally the Starlighter would catch a gust of wind and the control winglets would cap shut or snap open, and the ship would bob on a wave of air. Only a small amount of power went to keep the stabilizer ring spinning. The soft ringing hum and the rhythmic bouncing was unnerving.

"What do you think we should do?" asked Portia quietly.

"Well," said Bess, "if we can get close before they notice us, I say we glide in, turn on the power, and use your big Zap-Gun to take out the engines. If it can't fly, it can't fight."

Portia was quiet, still thinking. "That's a good idea," she said, softly but firmly.

Bess watched the light of the morning sun creep over the land. They were far from town and the two ships were closing fast. Bess looked down at the Crater, passing underneath her and far below. The shadows were creeping away and soon the light would illuminate the crashed and broken ray gun that was destroyed the night before. "What would they think when they saw that?"

As if on cue, the sunrise illuminated the rim of the Crater and Crescent Ridge. Sparkles of sunlight glinted off the broken metal and glass. A white circle of light appeared on the wreckage. Bess traced the beam back, and up. It appeared from underneath the quickly approaching space ship.

"Somethin's got them mad, you two. Be on the lookout," drawled Steve over the radio. Bess knew they had discovered the wrecked ray gun. It wouldn't take them long to figure they didn't have control over the air, or even the land.

It took only a moment for the space ship to respond. A green bast shot out from under the ship, targeting the road that led into Three Winds. The asphalt erupted into an explosion of black tar and white dust. The road was ripped from the bed for a hundred feet. The asphalt bubbled into a boiling tar. The rocks and sand were thrown into the air only to melt and turn to dirty glass. The space ship shuddered from the powerful blast.

The giant ray blast was only a few miles from the town. They would be able to target the homes and businesses within moments. Bess was shocked at the severity of the blast. This ship had weapons far more powerful than the smaller flying saucers she had chased on horseback. She leaned on the collective, angling the Starlighter to fall down through the sky like a knife cutting through the night.

"We're still too far off to use the Starlighter to disable their engines," Portia said. She was shocked at how loud she sounded, and how much her voice echoed in the tinny confines of the Starlighter's cockpit. The main engine still was silent. There was no heartbeat to the ship.

"If we power up," Bess said, "they will see us sooner. We can only hope we get close enough in time." They only needed a few more seconds. The Starlighter was whipping silently through the night sky on its edge toward the giant space ship. Bess willed the Starlighter forward as she twisted her hand tightly on the controls. She just needed to close the distance before they fired again.

As if to grind their heel into Bess's silent wishes, the space ship fired their ray gun at the first target that was close enough for them to hit. Outside of the town stood the small radio tower that broadcast music around Three Winds and the open prairie. A green ray crashed into the spindly metal frame. It sparked, bent, and glowed with the energy of the blast. Then the base collapsed under its own weight. The soft light of the radio sign, its call letters in a beautiful neon pastel, blinked and faded. The tower fell next to the building like an old and dead tree.

While Bess knew the station didn't come on before sunrise, she wasn't sure if anyone was inside. Jesse's father had the tower and station built, and she knew Jesse occasionally worked there. From far away, Bess could only barely see the radio station. She couldn't tell if there was a car there or not.

She only knew the moon men had taken one more thing from her and her friends. They wouldn't take any more. The Starlighter was close now, and they hadn't seen it or responded to it yet. She repowered the Starlighter with a hard punch to the power switch. The ship throbbed with power. The *thumpthumpthump* of the Starlighter pulsed through the metal and into the seats. It rapidly increased in speed as it flew toward the giant space ship. Bess scanned the huge upper surface. At a closer distance, she could make out details on it. The center had a set of large glass windows under a flattened dome of metal. Four bulges came out of the top, forming the corners of a square pattern on the circular saucer. Behind the big control dome, what must be the cockpit or helm, were two large circles covered in mesh grates. Behind them were large ducts. The air shimmered and changed over the weird circles. It looked like heat mirages on the desert, Bess thought, but even more strange. Bits of dust and rock were trapped in the waving air, as if gravity itself was turned off over the big ship. Bess remembered the moon man saying they used the Earth's gravity to fly their ships.

"Those big circles. Those are our targets."

At the high closing speeds, the two ships would cross in only seconds. It would allow for a small window for the Starlighter to strike the *Revenge*.

"We will need to be close," Portia said.

"How close?"

Portia wasn't sure how far the weapon on the Starighter would work. She had never tested it. "I don't know, two hundred feet? One hundred might be better."

"One hundred feet? That's going to be close."

Bess pushed on the collective. The Starlighter slowed and angled down, getting closer to the big space ship. As they got close to the *Revenge*, the domes across the top deck began to open. Four ray guns appeared from inside the domes and tried to track the fast moving Starlighter. As the Starlighter flew over the ship, the ray guns fired. They were unable to target the Starlighter as it tore across the top of the *Revenge*. Green rays of energy crisscrossed the morning sky, but they hit nothing.

Portia fired the static charge from the Starlighter. It worked like Bess's Zap-Gun. The center point that made the electric explosions that powered its flight filled with a huge static charge. The pent up energy popped out from the point of the Starlighter, shooting electricity out the discharge point. A burst of blue lightning ripped into the metal of the space ship. It crackled across the hull until it made contact with the strange engine intakes. The grating tore apart with a deafening explosion. The whole ship twisted and collapsed on one side before righting itself.

"Well, we got their attention now," Bess said. She pushed the throttle up to high speed, flying the Starlighter away from the *Revenge*. The big ship slowed. Bess could see the big repulsors on the bottom of the ship pushing into the ground to turn. Great clouds of dust and sand flew into the air, obscuring the giant saucer. But it did stop its progress toward Three Winds. The moon men now saw the Starlighter as a threat.

Bess whipped the Starlighter back around, zigzagging across the sky. The *Revenge* opened fire again with green beams shooting into the sky at the fast moving target. A close beam shook the Starlighter, sending it skewing sideways and falling. Bess pushed on the collective, righting the Starlighter. "We've got to stop those ray gun beams!" she yelled to her mother in the excitement of flying around the flashing blasts. "We can't be trying to dodge them all and use up all our power." Bess cranked the Starlighter into a tight flat turn that pushed her craft on its edge, and pushed Bess and Portia into their seats.

Portia moaned softly from the forces pushing her into her seat. Bess was used to the high gravity forces that pressed on a pilot when they flew, but her mother wasn't ready for a turn that tight. She didn't complain though. When she got her breath back, she asked, "What do you plan to do?"

"We're gonna come in low over them, and fast. I'll aim for the center, then flip just outside one set of those ray guns.

They can't swivel fast enough to track us. We can take out two in one pass." Hopefully, she didn't say out loud.

Bess lowered the Starlighter to almost even with the top of the *Revenge*. She poured on the speed but kept her angle as flat as possible. She didn't want the Starlighter to be an easy target. Coming in flat meant it was just a fast moving sliver, barely seen on its edge. She could see the upper ray guns, all four, try to lower down and point at her as she headed straight at the big saucer. As soon as she saw the bright glow from the first ray gun, she pushed hard right, just a flick, and then flattened back out as soon as she got over the saucer.

The saucer was a blur at that speed. Portia engaged the Starlighter's static charge, and blue flame poured out from underneath it. "We must be only forty feet apart," thought Bess. The blue beam was more like a rope than a lightning bolt at this range. It drug across the metal hull of the ship. Out from behind the Starlighter came a wake of metal, junk, smoke, and then, explosions. As she passed over the ray guns, large round pops of green light, huge bubbles of energy, exploded across the hull of the *Revenge*.

Bess pressed the throttle forward, hard. She wanted to escape any attempt of the moon saucer to fire back at her. Below her, now closer as both ships had changed altitude, lay Crescent Ridge, and the wreck of the big ray gun from the night before.

"Hold on!" was all the warning Bess could give. She pulled back on the throttle, opened all the control winglets, and threw the Starlighter into a hard braking maneuver, stopping it in mid-air before it began to float down.

A stray ray gun beam ripped through the morning sky, far off from the Starlighter, but very close to where it would have been if Bess had kept going. She dropped her ship below the ridge line. Then, at a more deliberate pace, began flying across the west side of the range of low mountains. "This will give us a little protection," Bess said. As she spoke, far behind them came an explosion on the other side of the mountains. A cloud of dust and rock flew into the sky, where the *Revenge* had blasted a hole into the mountainside. Portia said with relief, "Well, I think you made a good choice. I'm very happy we weren't there.

"Now, where will we be next?"

Bess tried to think. Another blast shook the mountains behind her. "They're trying to find us," she said.

Far ahead of her, she saw her opportunity. The mountains turned to the east, and there was a break in the ridge wall. "We're going through there," she told her mother.

Portia looked into the distance, then clenched her seat tightly. "Through that?!" The passage was a thin slit in the mountains. It was too small to pass through. "We'll never fit!" she cried.

"Not horizontally," Bess said. "We go through there, come around behind them, take out the rest of the ray guns, and then pour it on 'til their engines give out!"

"Or ours do," Portia gasped. "Or I do," she half whispered.

"Don't worry," Bess said, "we've got this, Mom. Those moon men won't know who hit them!"

CHAPTER 24

Battle In The Sky

Bess pushed the Starlighter to its limit. She swung out and slammed the ship onto its side. The winglets chattered as the high speed wind tried to push through the small gaps in the closed metal panels. The engine *thumpthumped* to keep the Starlighter flying on a knife's edge as Bess lined up to pass through the tiny gap between the mountain peaks.

Portia gasped, then held her breath, then just closed her eyes.

The Starlighter passed into, then through, the gap in a flash. It was through before Bess could even react. The ship burst out from behind the shadow of the mountains into the morning sun. It glinted in shiny chrome from the full light of dawn. To her left, the *Revenge* was tearing into the mountains far away. It was slowly rising to get above the ridge to keep hunting the Starlighter. The bright glint of polished metal caught the attention of the moon men in the cockpit. It slowed its rise in the air and began to slowly rotate toward the fast moving ship. A large ray shot out from under the ship, but it couldn't elevate high enough to hit the faster Starlighter. The beam tore up the open plains but never reached the quicker ship.

Bess threw the Starlighter into a wide loop. "Get ready, Mom!"

Portia finally opened her eyes. "We're still alive?" Bess wasn't sure if she was joking or not.

"Yes! Get ready!"

Bess looped the Starlighter around and began a wide pass toward the *Revenge*. As the big ship rose up, she passed along the thick rounded side of the saucer. The dull edge came up fast, and close. Portia engaged the Zap-Gun, and blue bolts tore into the side of the saucer. Explosions triggered off as more and more of the *Revenge* was damaged.

Bess leveled the Starlighter so she could fly higher and get away. She quickly cleared the mountains and headed for open sky. It was a rare moment of peace after a lot of stress. "How much power do we have left?" she asked as she took a few deep breaths.

"We better hurry," her mother answered. "We've got about ten minutes of flying time left, at this rate."

The entire ship shook with a horrifying crash. A ray beam impacted directly under the Starlighter. It immediately flew upwards from the impact. The engine shut down and the ship flew up to an apex, then it stopped at its zenith. For a quiet moment, the Starlighter was frozen in the air, neither rising nor falling. The entire ship had glazed over in a flash of green, then became silent. Even the outside wind was isolated from the cockpit.

Then it began to fall.

Bess had to check her body to see if it still worked. She didn't know if she had broken every bone in her body or if she was fine. The tremendous blast had stunned her. Then as the Starlighter fell, she felt her arms and legs lift. Her body floated softly in the straps of her seat. She had momentarily gone weightless as her body caught up with the falling Starlighter all around her.

She gathered her wits as she realized she was falling. Getting her arms under control, she punched the power switch a moment before Portia reached for the same control at her station. There was a quiet moment where nothing happened. A cold fear of terror raced across Bess's body. If she couldn't get the Starlighter refired ...

Thumthumthump went the heartbeat. They were back under power. Bess twisted the throttle, and pushed the collective, sending the ship into a slow dive to escape the next ray gun blast.

"Now we've got five minutes," Portia's voice was surprisingly calm for just being shot out of the sky. "That beam just took half our energy."

"And I think it cooked our stabilizer," Bess added. The outer ring that spun at high speed was now humming with a very irritating whine.

"I think the blast hit us dead underneath. It is made to withstand the controlled explosions of the electrical charge.

It may have overheated us and the ring. It may be a little too tight to fit well now," Portia explained.

"She still flies okay," Bess said as she wiggled the collective, sending the Starlighter into small banks left and right.

A deep squawk of static came from the formerly silent radio. "You two alright?" came Steve Truly's voice.

"Yes," Bess responded, "We're alright, just got a little cooked back there. Starlighter's holding together. Over."

"Just so ya know," Steve drawled, "you got fast movers coming in from Holloman, ten minutes."

"Roger," answered Bess, "just make sure they know the small one is the good guys." Steve had alerted Bess that fighter planes would be coming in from Holloman Air Force base. "Over and Out."

Bess had a chance to think about the planes. "We need to clear the skies for those planes, Mom. If those fighters come in and those ray guns are still active, they'll pick off the planes one by one. They can't manoeuvre like we can."

"Well," replied Portia firmly, "we better do something about that." Portia was sore and a little shaken from the flight, but she wasn't about to let anyone else finish what she and Bess had started.

"Alright," Bess swooped back around. She kept the Starlighter low so that the ray guns wouldn't be able to shoot at her as she came over the mountain range once more. "We're going to come up on them quick. They have been trying to track us as we fly by, but this time we're going to stop short. I'm gonna jam up their ray guns when they think we are going to fly over, stop right on top of them, and then we take the ray guns out."

Without waiting for an answer, Bess pushed the Starlighter forward at high speed. She had only moments left, with little power. If this didn't work, and they ran out of electricity, the Starlighter would stop in the air and drift down. It would be a sitting duck for the moon men's ray guns. She couldn't cut and run, or go land the Starlighter. If no one stopped the big flying saucer, it would rip her town to shreds with the ray guns, and come after her home. Bess didn't have any choice. Even if she did, this would be the one she would make. She readied herself for the attack.

Aiming for the very top of Crescent Ridge, Bess flew forward. At the last moment, she lifted the Starlighter, twisting up the throttle to add lift, and bounced over the line of the ridge. The *Revenge* loomed large right in front of her. In the few seconds of closing speed, the ray guns slowly tried to turn toward the Starlighter to track it and fire upon it. They immediately began pointing up, moving away from her even as the big ship tried to slow and turn toward the attack. The ray guns were hoping to catch the quick Starlighter just as it passed over the ship, and blast the little craft from the sky. That was just what Bess wanted.

As soon as she crossed over the edge of the saucer's hull, Bess threw the Starlighter into a hard stop, with the engine thumping away to quickly slow the ship. It hung almost motionless over the edge of the *Revenge*, floating, and waiting. Bess saw clearly for a fleeting moment the moon men staring out the damaged windows of the large central helm. The two remaining ray guns still moved away from her, and then fired. Twin beams of green energy, lights filled with hate and destruction, shot out into the morning sky. They flew up, harmless and useless, hitting nothing. The moon men looked on in horror. They knew they had missed, and missed badly. The Starlighter hovered only forty feet above the scarred and damaged hull. Bess wondered if the moon men could see her from their view. They would have seen a glorious and gleaming smile.

The static charge from the Starlighter engaged, crashing into the metal. Bess pressed her ship forward. The Zap-Gun ripped the first ray gun to bits, twisting the metal to an unrecognizable mess. The beam tore in deeper and deeper into the hull, until it crossed the other ray gun, still pointed up and away. It moved, but too slowly to even get close to aiming at the Starlighter. The blue lightning ripped at the ray gun's base. It simply tore the ray gun from the ship. It folded and flopped onto the outer hull, lifeless and broken.

Bess lifted up over the *Revenge*. Now that the saucer had lost all its ray guns on the top deck, it was almost impossible for the big ship to fight back. It's port engine was smoking and torn. There were numerous holes in the hull and cockpit. The only functional ray guns were on the bottom deck. The ship was too low to fire outside the line of Crescent Ridge, and it couldn't lift well enough to get clear of the mountains.

"We're almost done, Sweetie," said Portia. She felt a little more calm now that the ray guns weren't shooting at her. But they only had minutes left to fly, and the big moon saucer was still a threat.

"One more shot," said Bess. "Let's hit that other engine."

She flew over the starboard engine duct. In the strange gravity well that powered the ship, there was a wavy orbit of rocks, dust, and shards of broken metal from the damage done to the *Revenge*. Portia engaged the Zap-Gun, with one final blast. The blue flame sparked and ripped into the big metal grate. It tore open and the entire ship dipped with an audible metallic sigh.

Immediately, a loud chime rang through the Starlighter. Bess knew what it meant. "Off, Mom," she commanded. She didn't have time to explain. Bess pushed the throttle up and the Starlighter took off into the air. She leaned the collective forward. Her ship leaned with it as it was pointed toward the west, with Three Winds and the C Bar M directly ahead, but far away.

"Bingo!" Bess yelled, then pressed the radio button. "We're out of fuel, Dad, coming in, we might be gliding."

Her father responded after a moment. "Good job, kiddo! And just in time. Those fighters are coming in fast. Get clear as best you can. Over."

"Two minutes, dear," said Portia softly.

"That's, well, that's enough to get outta Dodge," Bess finally had a moment to look at her mother and grin. "We can get home on that. We may come in quiet, but we should make it to the strip." Her mother hadn't experienced any part of flying the Starlighter before. Now she was going to go through a powerless spiral landing. Bess was already a pro at it. This would be the second time she would have to float down from the sky.

A minute later, another buzzer went off. Portia pressed a button to silence it. "We're almost out," she said.

The two sat quietly. There wasn't much to say. They both glanced back at the smoking hulk of the *Revenge*. It still tried to lift and move, but struggled, like a ship stuck on a sandbar. There wasn't anything left for Bess to do. She hoped the Army and Air Force could finally bring the saucer down.

As if on cue, two things happened. To the south, she saw tiny glints of light. Little blinking stars winked on for a moment in the southern horizon. The fighters from Holloman had shown up.

Then the Starlighter went silent.

The heartbeat stopped, and again, for a moment, the ship floated silently and softly in the sky. Bess, almost casually, grabbed the release handle and pulled the winglets halfway open. The Starlighter caught the morning winds coming from the west. It slowed and started to spin softly. Far below and ahead stretched out the C Bar M airstrip.

Bess felt her body go soft for a moment. She breathed in and out deeply. Her hands relaxed on the controls. The ship would almost land itself. She was tired and ready for

200

about a day's sleep. It took a few minutes to get the Starlighter into landing position. It simply hovered down and forward through the soft morning air.

She was still about a minute away from her home when there was a distant rumble, as smoke billowed over Crescent Ridge. The fighter jets had finished in bringing down the *Revenge*. Bess barely noticed.

"Coming in soft," Bess called to her father over the radio. He didn't answer, because she saw a tall thin cowboy with his arm in a sling waving a hat in the air out on the tarmac.

Bess twisted the collective slightly. The Starlighter slowed, straightened, and fell gently toward the airstrip. A cushion of air fluffed up under the ship's bottom chamber, then with a soft exhale, the Starlighter touched down on the ground.

"Any landing you can walk away from," Bess said.

CHAPTER 25

The Round-Up

It had been a month since the events of the invasion from the moon. The rest of the town had breathed a collective sigh of relief on the day after the invasion, but Bess simply slept through the night. It took several days to even start to get back to normal, but school had restarted, and if anything had a way of equalizing the kids in town, it was final exams.

The road into town had been destroyed by the moon men, and it had been the last thing to be fixed. The roads from the south and west had still been open, technically, but they were greatly restricted. Agent Marsh had explained that they didn't want too many people coming in to look at all the damage. Portia suggested, "You could be trying to cover all this up, couldn't you?"

Agent Marsh had responded cryptically, "We're not going to keep this from anyone, Dr. Truly. However, there's nothing that says we are going to make this easy for them."

Bess commented after everything was over that Agent Marsh came through this all without even getting a gray hair on his head. Weeks later, when the two agents were finally leaving, she mentioned, "You knew their language." She asked, "You've dealt with them before, haven't you?" Marsh just walked toward his airplane with Agent Phillips in tow. He turned back, smiled and gave a shrug that didn't confirm anything, but made Bess feel she was right about him. "He didn't even get his suit wrinkled."

Bess figured it was just as well that no one was coming from out of town to see the damage. She, Aurora, Lydia, and Jesse had all gone out the next few days after the crash to watch the Army take apart the saucer and cart it away on big trucks. "No one would believe us anyway," she said. Aurora took a picture and said, "Yeah, but we'll know."

Lydia tried to compromise. "We don't need this to become a tourist stop. I like Three Winds like it is, nice and quiet."

The girls giggled, and Jesse snickered at the joke. "One thing's for sure, stuff like this will never happen to us again!"

It took time to rebuild the road. Other things happened much faster. Mr. Armstrong's radio tower was carted off, and a new one started going up within the same day. It was new, and tall, and the music came out static free for miles.

The C Bar M had a large cleanup from the plane crash. The airstrip was extended with temporary metal plates, then big concrete slabs were poured to handle the large planes that landed there regularly. The ranch was used as a supply base for the military to unload equipment and load pieces of the giant flying saucer and its smaller counterparts. Some of the G-men that showed up, as well as military, suggested that the Truly family move out of their home while these secretive devices roll through the property. This talk was stopped in its tracks by both Agents Marsh and Phillips, who pointed out that Portia Truly probably knew more about the atomic aspects of the moon weapons than the people carting them off. The soldiers had remained on the site, camping out in the open hangars. Captain Brooks, and many of the ground troops, stopped any talk about Bess, pointing out that she was the one who took down all the saucers. No one was going to say a word about her being out on her own ranch. All the Army soldiers kept their mouths shut, even when they realized they were the guests of an Air Corps pilot.

Electra became a bit of hero, as well. She received so much attention in her stall that Corporal Robinson had to station a guard to keep curious soldiers from bothering her or bringing her treats.

The more difficult issues included dealing with the moon men. Agent Marsh had explained to the Truly family that he was able to interrogate many of the captured moon men. Due to them continually handling radioactive material on the moon, their environment had become toxic. They had ruined the subterranean dwellings where they lived, hidden just beneath the surface, with radioactivity. Many people had gone deeper down, separating themselves from others to keep away from the radioactivity and disease that permeated the moon's surface. A few hundred men had decided to use the last of their ships to invade the Earth, in hopes of spreading enough damage and radiation that the Earthlings could not fight back.

Bess had snickered at the idea, "It didn't work out well for them." Her mother, however, knew well the dangers of radiation, and how much of a risk they had just averted. "It could have been much, much worse."

Portia had been able to study some of the treatments the moon men used to treat their radioactivity, especially the strange pills that helped sweat out toxins from deep within their bones. She hoped it would help with treatment on Earth as well.

The moon men had all been captured. While many were injured from the defense of Three Winds and the crash of the *Revenge*, all had survived. Corporal Robinson had explained to Bess, "We really don't want to kill them. I mean," he shrugged, "we, well, we'd prefer to be bored, not even doing this, but... Those guys are extremely radioactive at close range, and they'd give off a lot of radiation if they die. They'd be like big glowing radioactive slugs. This way, we can capture them and move them to a safer place." Bess didn't ask where they were taken, and she wouldn't have been told, anyway. Corporal Robinson did say that since they were no longer handling radioactive materials, they may get better, due to their treatment and medicines. "They will be somewhere like their home on the moon." Bess thought about how the moon is dry, dusty, hot and bright. "Kinda

206

like here," she thought out loud. Corporal Robinson said nothing, but gave her a knowing wink.

James Fields fared even less well. He was a traitor to his country, and to the world. He had been sentenced to prison. He didn't even argue it. He pled guilty and went straight to jail. Bess felt bad for Nanette. She may or may not have known what he had been doing, but it wasn't like she had planned everything, or wanted her home invaded by aliens and half destroyed. The ranch had to be sold to a large dairy company. Nanette and her mother had to move into a smaller home in town.

Jesse and his father were decidedly torn over the events. It had been shocking with all that had happened. But Mr. Armstrong got a new radio tower out of it, and made a deal with the dairy farm to make local specialty ice cream for his soda shop every week. Jesse also got a girlfriend when Annie Perez actually asked him out to the movies. Jesse was surprised at the film. "You want to see *The Black Sleep*?! You like horror films?" Aurora teased Jesse mercilessly that week. "Ha! You're gonna be so scared, Annie will have hold *your* hand!"

So things changed, things got moved, and things got fixed. Some things didn't get fixed, like the scars and damage to the mountains and land done by the big ray gun beams. Weather and time would slowly heal most of the wounds, though they would remain visible for years to keen eyes. But the town moved forward.

June came on hot and dry. School finished for everyone. Bess and the rest of the Zap-Gun Rangers all went through exams feeling comfortable that they did well. Aurora worried about getting a B in algebra, while Lydia worried she might have missed one question in English. Bess just looked forward to summer and time off. Jesse didn't worry about anything.

As soon as school ended, the kids got together with some of the cowboys from the C Bar M and threw a big rodeo. It wasn't a fancy, organized event. It was simple, but big. Everyone showed up. It was a chance for the kids in town to show off their horses and hang out. Bess and Aurora had made bright blue ribbons for their horses, and then decided to make enough for anyone who wanted them. It became a symbol for the rodeo. The ribbons were tied into the manes of the horses and around the ponytails of many of the kids that were there.

Bess entered Electra into a highly contested barrel race. They ran well together. Electra was quick and tight with her turns, accelerating away from the barrels with no need for encouragement. But Bess could tell that Electra wasn't going as fast as she could. Aurora's horse ended up winning the race. Her black and white paint horse ran with wild abandon, snorting the air while digging in hard with her hooves. Aurora was as surprised as everyone else. She patted her horse down as she brushed her, "I guess she didn't want to be left out of all this attention!"

Annie and Jesse saw Bess washing down Electra after the race. Annie asked, "Didn't you think your horse would win?" Annie stroked Electra's neck while feeding her a handful of oats.

"Oh, no. Not really," Bess answered. "To be honest, I think after all the events of the past month, Electra here just doesn't get excited over something as simple as a barrel race. Anyway, Aurora won, fair and square. We couldn't have beat her after the ride she had."

Annie thought that was nice of Bess, to be honest about the results and to give credit to her friend. It was something new for her to see. She hadn't been around Bess and her friends very often, not without Nanette.

"I wish you could have gotten Nanette to come," Bess told her.

"I know. I tried," Annie answered. "We'll give her time."

Jesse grinned, "And give her some ice cream. Ice cream always helps."

Annie squeezed Jesse's shoulder and shook him softly. "Hey, why weren't you out there? Don't you ride a horse?"

Jesse and Bess laughed. "I'm more into horsepower than horses," he joked. "I'll tell you what, after they are done out there, I'll take you out in the Desert Cadillac and we can do figure eights in the dirt."

"You do that and you'll scare all the horses within twenty miles!" came a voice from the door to the stables. Aurora grinned at Jesse as she and Lydia led their horses into

209

the shade of the stalls. Another horse walked in with them, led by a young girl in a big white hat and very scuffed up boots.

"Hey, Bess, we got someone who wanted to meet you, and Electra. This," said Lydia, as she made room for the girl and her horse, "is Talia."

Bess looked at Talia, who was probably a very confident seven years old. Under her big hat, wild curly hair stuck out, all red and twisted into messy flames of fire. A toothy grin with a single gap shone white from her mouth, and freckles covered her brown cheeks. She led a beautiful chestnut mare with a ribbon on the saddle. "Hi, Talia, I'm Bess. These are our friends, Annie and Jesse. I guess you already know Aurora and Lydia. And who is this?" Bess stroked Talia's horse.

"This is my horse, Tessla," she said proudly.

Bess looked at the ribbon on the saddle. "What did you win?"

"We got second place in barrel riding in my age group," Talia said, standing tall in her boots.

"Talia said she wanted to meet you and Electra," explained Lydia. "We just had to make that happen."

"Yeah," continued Talia. "I just wanted to say, thanks for what you did for us. I want to be just like you when I grow up!"

Bess knelt down to look Talia in the eyes. On one knee, Bess was just an inch shorter than the young girl. She took her hat off so Talia could see her face and eyes. "Thanks, cowgirl.

"But listen. You don't need to grow up to be just like me. It's important to be brave and confident. That's something great to have in your heart. But it's also important to be curious," she looked at Aurora.

"Or adventurous," she moved her eyes to Lydia.

"Or generous," she looked at Jesse.

"Or kind," Bess glanced to Annie, who smiled back in appreciation.

"But the most important part is this," Bess searched for the words Talia would understand. "You grow up to be who you want to be."

She stood up and stretched. Bess looked at her friends, old and new, gathered together.

"Now, let's go for a ride."

About The Author

Joe Sledge is the author of the Did You See That? North Carolina travel series of books. A native of North Carolina, his love of travel and exploration sent him across the county by car, airplane, or boat. On his first trip to the West Coast, Joe became fascinated with the deserts and plains along Route 66, along with the cultural history so prevalent to the area, which was so different than the coast of NC.

With a love of old time science fiction, an amateur study of Cold War era events, as guided by tales from his father, and a desire to write a book series that would appeal to his daughter, and kids anywhere, Joe created Bess Truly, an adventurous teen with a fast horse and a quick draw.

Joe currently resides in North Carolina with his wife and daughter.